Virginia Wales Johnson

The Kettle Club

Christmas Tales for Children

Virginia Wales Johnson

The Kettle Club
Christmas Tales for Children

ISBN/EAN: 9783337025380

Printed in Europe, USA, Canada, Australia, Japan

Cover: Foto ©Andreas Hilbeck / pixelio.de

More available books at **www.hansebooks.com**

THE KETTLE CLUB.

CHRISTMAS TALES FOR CHILDREN.

BY

COUSIN VIRGINIA.

BOSTON:

NICHOLS AND NOYES.

1866.

CAMBRIDGE:

STEREOTYPED AND PRINTED BY JOHN WILSON AND SON.

TO

Frank and Baby

THIS LITTLE BOOK IS AFFECTIONATELY DEDICATED,

BY THE AUTHOR.

CONTENTS.

———◆———

THE KETTLE CLUB.

EVENING had come. The snow lay spread over hill and valley in soft, white masses, the stars twinkled merrily in the clear, cold sky, and the icicles hung in fringes from the eaves, like so many crystals.

A large, comfortable farmhouse was nestled against a steep hill, as if for protection from the sharp, biting wind, and, if you would like a pleasant glimpse of the interior, just peep through the window with me into the cheerful, old-fashioned kitchen, with its heavy beams, wooden settle in the chimney-corner, and open hearth with huge, blazing logs upon it.

Do you see the strings of dried apples festooned across the ceiling, and the squash seeds upon the

[7]

mantel-piece, and the ears of corn ready to parch, in a merry company?

Do you notice that Hulda, the maid-servant, with her sleeves rolled up, is skimming the cream off great shining pans of milk in the dairy, to get every thing ready for an early churning to-morrow? And do you know that Zedekiah, the man-servant, is looking after the pretty brown calves, and pigs in the barn-yard, that they may have nice, warm beds this cold night?

You may wonder that none of the family enjoyed the warm kitchen, but they are all off on a frolic of a sleigh-ride, so, if you were some miles away, the tinkle of their bells might be heard.

Now I will draw the curtain, if you please, that the Saucepan, Cricket, Kettle and Teapot may have affairs their own way, without the inter-ference of strangers.

WHAT THE SAUCEPAN DID.

——◆——

A FAT little Saucepan sat among the coals, with something very good, to judge by the savory smell, cooking inside of it.

"Oh, dear me!" it sputtered hotly, "where's the use of living, if one must be kept on a red hot bed of coals until nearly melted, in this way. I am no sooner scraped and rubbed into a fine state of polish, by the maid and set upon the shelf to cool myself a bit, than whisk! somebody comes along, spies me doing nothing, and I am on the fire again, stewing away for dear life.

"It is all nonsense, I say, that people must have hot suppers, for I am sure I never ate a thing in all my life, and just see, for all that, how plump I am. Besides, there should be another of my size to let me have some rest, instead of working all the time. Well, there is one comfort in

1*

it all : I shall be worn out sometime, for I have already been sent to the tinman because of holes, and then I shall be allowed to rust to pieces and die, I suppose.

"Bubble, bubble, sputter, sputter, hiss, fiss!" puffed the Saucepan, indignant at its own wrongs.

"Still," it added loftily, "I would not exchange places with any one. As for you, friend Cricket, it is well that you have so good a temper and are content with very little. I am sure, were I a live animal, with four legs, you would not find me staying on a poky old hearth all this time. No! I would go out into the world to see every thing new and delightful. I would visit cities, to look up at the great church-steeples, or I would creep to the top of some forest tree to see the ocean and the ships sailing away. However, as it is, I would rather be a Saucepan, for I am surely of more importance than *you*. Friend Kettle, you seem to be also of rather a dull nature, if you will excuse my saying so. I have never seen you at all excited: you just swing from your hook over the fire all day long, and simmer placidly. I cannot but pride myself that I have more spirit, that I know when I am imposed upon better than you do, for you never utter a word of complaint.

"In addition to having sometimes a moment of rest upon the shelf, I am a much smaller figure and lighter build, so I would prefer being a Saucepan to *you*.

"Bless me, bubble, hiss, fiss! I would not change places with you, Madam Teapot, for any thing you could mention, although you do think yourself very fine, I know, — quite above a common chit of a Saucepan like me, — but let me tell you, I would like to be exactly what I am, never having seen any thing better than a pedler's wagon, where I was exchanged for a bundle of rags, than you with all the bright colors painted on your sides, for your nose is badly broken, and your handle cracked, while I, thank fortune, am whole, and a pretty little body enough for most people, I hope."

At all this the Cricket chirruped scornfully, while the old Kettle only laughed in a fat way, inside of itself, for it was infinitely amused at the conceit of the arrogant little Saucepan ; and as for the Teapot, it was **so** angry at being snubbed in this way, that **it sent a** spout of tea **out of the** broken **nose.**

Now the hot-tempered Saucepan enjoyed **the** evident chagrin of the Cricket **and** Teapot, but it **no** sooner heard **the low,** chuckling laugh of the Kettle above its head, than, puffing with wrath — what do **you** suppose it did ?—why, it boiled **over.**

WHAT THE CRICKET THOUGHT.

——◆——

"PERHAPS you will be kind enough to listen to me for a moment," chirped the Cricket politely, "as we have nothing to do this evening but enjoy ourselves together —— ."

"Have we not, indeed!" interrupted the Saucepan, in a more peppery state than ever, since it had boiled over. "It seems to me that I am pretty hard at work, for one; however, go on, as you have no cooking to do."

"It is rude to interrupt," bubbled the Kettle.

"What can you expect for manners from a Saucepan?" hissed the Teapot spitefully.

"Well, well, friends," interposed the good-natured Cricket, "we will not mind trifles, as the Saucepan has got into a heat. I have been thinking of telling you my adventures, for I am now old, and have seen a good deal in my day, although you all suppose I have never wandered from the hearth."

" We should be most happy to hear you," said the Kettle courteously.

" Very much so indeed ! " added the Teapot graciously.

" To be sure," echoed the Saucepan, rather ashamed of itself.

" I was born here," continued the Cricket, placing himself at his ease upon a hot brick, and warming one foot at the blaze while he spoke. " We were a very large family, and, I do not deny, a very poor one also, for our father and mother had to work hard enough to find insects, when we were too young to help them. That is the worst of being a Cricket, one must eat, or die. So far from doing nothing, as you have supposed, I have to poke about everywhere to find my dinner, and sometimes it runs away from me into a crack or cranny even then.

" I was rather a wild youngster, I fear, much more fond of toasting myself at the fire, than getting my living. The heavy smoke rolling up chimney in clouds, with darting flames curling through the masses, had great attractions for me. I saw in the burning embers such wonderful things! First the coals would appear like a beautiful castle, with towers and parapets, then they changed to gardens of graceful trees and moving forms. Oh! I could fancy faces: now that of a fat old lady, with puffing cheeks, and feathers on her head, then some queer little elf, who would wink at me, cut a caper, and vanish. I still see pictures in the fire, but I am older now, and they do not dazzle me as they did once.

"At last my parents talked together about my singular conduct. My brothers and sisters were already hunting their own spiders, while I sat all day staring at the fire, and cared very little whether I ate or not.

"'My dear, what ails him?' said my father.

"'I have no doubt but that his stomach is disordered, so I will make him some medicine for a tonic,' replied my mother wisely.

"So she set about preparing her tonic. Having killed a nice large spider herself, she cut off two legs, dried and grated them to a fine powder; next she added a few gnat's-wings and a fly's head; she then put the whole, with a drop of water and a pinch of ashes, into a hickory nutshell and cooked it over the fire, when the family were asleep. This is really a very good medicine indeed, and I have frequently taken it since, especially in the spring, when one loses appetite, but at the time I mention it did no good.

"'Well,' said my father a second time, 'what ails him?'

"'Really!' exclaimed my mother, vexed that her favorite medicine should fail, 'I think our son crazy or a fool, which is all the worse, for I had hoped the children might have common sense at least.'

"'No,' replied my father, 'I believe he is a poet, which is certainly better than being a fool or crazy.'

"Although I did not prove to be a poet, as my father had expected, I did something quite as strange for a house-cricket, — I became a traveller. I thought of it for a long time, and the fire-pictures seemed to teach me what I should see when I left this quiet corner. So I announced my intention of leaving home, and, as I never had done any thing for myself, nobody cared much, while my mother was still provoked, that neither her medicine availed, nor I became a poet.

"I set forth, and was soon out all alone in the great world. At first I felt half afraid, the earth looked so large, the sky so high and grand, but then I encouraged myself to bravery by thinking of the fine times in store, able as I was to go where I pleased. 'First I will visit a great city,' said I, 'and after I have seen all the wonders there, I can go on to the ends of the earth if I choose.' But how could I find the way without any guide-book? Presently I saw a pond before me. I approached it cautiously, and beheld a huge bull-frog seated upon a broad leaf that floated upon the surface. I had never seen such a green monster in all my life, and, while I was gazing at him with all my eyes, he inflated his throat, and gave a hoarse croak! croak! I was half frightened out of my senses by the noise, and had hopped back a pace, when I saw a gay dragon-fly come dancing over the water towards me.

"'Will you please tell me the road to town?' I said.

" Just then a beautiful, speckled fish leaped up and swallowed the dragon-fly, then espying me upon the bank, it swam towards me.

" ' The road to town is right across this pond. All you have to do is to swim a bit, and you will soon be there,' said the fish in a soft, coaxing voice.

" ' Ho! ho!' laughed the bull-frog, jumping from his seat, and paddling nearer to me. ' The fish wants to eat you up. I will show you a' better way.'

" So saying, he opened wide his mouth and made a snap at me, but I skipped back as fast as my legs would carry me, and never paused until I had reached a stone, under which I hid. I had half a mind to turn homeward again, but I feared they would all laugh at me. I crept up a hill and down the other side, into a valley, where there was a great wood of trees and shrubs. I was so tired and hungry, that I did not know what to do next, and began to think it not so fine to travel after all, when, to my great joy, I saw two beetles at work near by. I told them my story, and begged for food and shelter, as they are relatives of the cricket tribe.

"'Just rest yourself on the moss there, until we get this bird buried,' said the sexton-beetle gruffly, but kindly, 'then we will see to you.'

"I sat down and watched them drag the bird to the brink of a little grave which they had dug for him, then spread the earth over neatly, and it all seemed very curious to me.

"'Now,' said the sexton-beetle when they had finished, 'come along, for I am hungry after all this work.'

"He presented me to his family, who all treated me kindly, and I was soon asleep in the best bedroom, which consisted of a cranny in an old tree-stump. The next day I felt so much better, that I started again on my journey, after having received directions from the father-beetle, as to which route to take.

"'I will go with you to the edge of the wood, and see if there is any business for me there,' said he.

"Bidding him good-by, I went on once more. I had not proceeded far, when I saw something gliding towards me, in the tall grass. Fearing that this object might want me for dinner after the manner of the bull-frog, I turned hastily to find some place of concealment, and discovered a partridge's nest, with all the pretty eggs exposed, for the mother must have left them for a moment. I ran with all speed to squeeze myself under this nest, and the other came straight towards me. It was a green-striped snake, which coiled itself about so that it touched me with the many folds of its slimy body. I shivered with fear, but I soon found it was the eggs, not me, that it wanted, and which it broke and sucked with great relish.

"I breathed a sigh of relief at my own safety, although I was very sorry that the poor bird should have her brood thus destroyed. The snake had not finished its meal, when the partridge came fluttering back, and, with a clamor of distress, even dared to attack the cruel foe in her despair. Quite a combat raged over my head, the bird flapping her wings, and the snake hissing defiance, until the latter glided away again, and I was left to resume my journey.

"I went by the meadows all day, and, as the sun shone pleasantly, I enjoyed it very much.

Towards dusk I noticed that a fine highway ran in the same direction, so I crept through a chink in the stone wall to try a change. But I soon repented of my folly.

" I heard a rushing, whirling, grinding sound behind me, that startled every sense I had out of my head, and soon there came dashing along a horse and carriage. Now, I dare say, this may seem very silly, but perhaps if you had been only a house-cricket, used to a quiet life, with the other frights for losing your life I had had already, you would have trembled at the thunder of a horse's hoofs. I determined to get into the field again, as soon as possible, when, to my dismay, a lady with a red cloak came mincing along, and the bright colors so enraged a band of geese, that they charged down upon her, their wings spread, their bills in the air, and all making so fearful a clamor, that no wonder she ran away. I ran away too, you had better believe, for I saw that a gosling already had his eye upon me, and would speedily devour my small body. In my terror I crawled down a hole, which proved to be the home of a horde of rats.

"The gosling thrust his beak in after me, but fortunately I was beyond his reach.

"'Wheugh! Heugh!' cried the grandfather rat, 'my whiskers tell me something nice is near.'

"So all the rat grandchildren began to snuff and sniff, until they found me, and I was as much afraid to remain in the hole as to leave it. Just as I ran out, a dog caught a glimpse of the first rat's nose poked up after me, and he began to scratch after it so fiercely, that they were glad enough to hide, and let me alone. Oh, what a sad night that was for me! It gives me a pain in my shoulder only to think of it. The rain began to fall, and I had never had my coat wet before. When the darkness came on, I was glad to take refuge under a mushroom from the storm. I could not sleep a wink, it was so cold. I tried to cover myself with blades of grass, but it was no use, they felt so stiff and sharp. With the daybreak I plodded on, without much hope of ever finding any thing pleasant.

"I was destined for better luck this time, however, for I came upon a land of grasshoppers, and a right merry set of fellows they are too. They hop, chirp, and dance all day long, without ever a thought or care, although they may be gobbled alive by some stray turkey the next moment. They soon made me feel gay again, and cordially invited me to live with them always. At first I considered this plan delightful; they had plenty to eat, they had nothing to do but dance, they were not in danger of snapping fish, why should I not stay?

"Alas! I soon saw that even a grasshopper's life is not all roses.

"A bustling old hen, with a family of chickens trotting after her, came among us, and, teaching the chicks to follow her example, she began to peck at us in the most savage manner. My heart sank within me, when I saw her sharp bill pushed through the stubble, and even snap up a poor little friend crouching beside me. I felt sure she would eat a cricket as readily as a grasshopper, so I closed my eyes, and awaited my fate.

"Just as she prepared to devour me, a lean gray cat came stealing along, and seized one of the chickens in her mouth. The old hen turned, flew at the marauder, and furiously pecked her eyes, so the cat dropped the chicken and fled. I made the most of my chance and escaped, never to return to the grasshopper community again, I hope.

"I could now see the city in the distance, so I determined to go forward and gratify my curiosity with its wonders. At last, I entered the streets, and never shall I forget my astonishment when I saw the tall houses rise above me, and the church steeples piercing the very sky, it seemed to me, and heard the sound of bells, machinery, and voices mingled together. I had to keep my wits about me, or I should have been crushed to death by the tramp of many feet upon the hard pavement. I searched about for a suitable dwelling, and finally selected the crack of a window in a lawyer's office, where I determined to stay long enough to see the world. This was the happiest part of all my wanderings, for, although I was exposed to many dangers, I had become used to them, and was not quite so nervous as when I left home.

"I went up the steeples of this great city, friend Saucepan, and explored the roofs, the chimneys, and so down to the cellars, though frequently in peril from the house-maid's broom.

"Finally I grew really tired of all the noise and bustle about me. 'If I was only home,' I sighed. 'However, I may as well go further now, and see the ocean once, then I shall rest content.' I left the city, and after having a bird pounce upon me, being nearly flattened to a wafer under a boy's boot, and narrowly escaping death from a toad, I reached a large wood, where I looked about in vain for the sea.

"'Hullo!' said a cheerful voice above me, and, upon looking in the direction of the sound, I saw upon a tree a handsome cousin of mine, the locust, all dressed in shining green armor.

"'Do come up and see us,' he continued. 'You look very tired. What are the news your way?'

"'I am just from town,' said I, with a fashionable air. 'It seems charming to see the country again.'

"'Been in the city,—eh?' returned the gay-hearted locust. 'Well, well, we are not very fashionable up here in the tree-tops, but we will

2

give you as fine a concert as most people to-night.'

"Sure enough, at twilight they began, and such music I never have heard. I can scrape a decent tune, I pride myself, but I cannot hold a candle to my cousins, the locusts. They sang duets from different trees, — 'Katy did,' 'Katy didn't;' then they chirped all together, and the tree-frogs trilled in, now and then, in the most beautiful manner, until I was perfectly wild with delight. I scraped my own legs, I leaped up in the air, I danced round and round, and should have fallen to the ground, had not a prudent old locust warned me of my danger.

"Next day, the party of friends escorted me to a very high tree, from the top of which we could see the broad ocean. There were the beautiful ships, with the full white sails set, sailing away like birds, and the waters rippling and sparkling in the sunlight dazzled my eyes with their splendor. Oh, how small and insignificant I felt when I saw the sea, that washes the shores of so many distant lands! yet I knew that the good God, who held these mighty waters in his grasp, had made me, a little cricket, as well.

"I will not tell you any more of my adventures now, for fear of tiring you. Having seen all the wonders of the world, I was glad enough to get home again, for I found myself happiest in the chimney-corner, after all. My parents were dead, my brothers and sisters married, so I took up my abode, and have lived here ever since, an old bachelor. When you were exclaiming upon your hard lot, my dear Saucepan, I could not refrain from giving my little experience in life, to show you, as far as was in my power, that we all have the place assigned us by God.

"This is what I thought," concluded the Cricket, with a chirp, chirp of satisfaction.

"We are very much obliged," simmered the Kettle, when he had finished.

"Yes, it was very interesting," said the Teapot.

"I really beg your pardon," said the Saucepan, "for I had no idea before that you were so wise and important a person."

WHAT THE KETTLE SAID.

—◆—

"TAKE life easy, friends," said the Kettle, in jolly tones. "Where is the use of fretting over things one cannot possibly help? Now I might say, swinging here on my hook, that I would manage affairs differently out in the world, if I could, but I cannot, so what good does it do? I might say, if I was lord of the whole earth, instead of an old smoke-blackened kettle, I would have all the people happy; there should be no sorrow or poverty, no hunger or cold. No, the world should be one beautiful garden of sweet flowers, delicious fruits, and waving trees, where the little birds might perch without fear of any foes, where the fierce lions and tigers might be tamed of their evil passions, and great serpents in frosted, glittering armor might be humbled from their venomous power. All these nice things

I should certainly try to do, if my strength was as great as my will, and it is all very pleasant to think of while boiling over the fire; but I also know that the Lord of the earth is much wiser than I am, and therefore it is his will that the savage animals crouch in the forests and tangled jungles for their food, and the snakes twine about trees under cover of the broad leaves to dart upon their prey.

"I can tell you nothing wonderful or interesting this evening, I fear, for I have had no adventures like our distinguished Cricket here, nor can I work myself into a steaming passion like the Saucepan, which is certainly very amusing to my mind. I have never been able to travel, although I have often desired to do so, for how can a Kettle go anywhere without being carried? To be sure, I have four legs, but they are so small you can scarcely see them, and they are of no manner of use to me, that I ever found out, for they seldom reach the ground, but are generally dangling in the air. I have known many changes in my time, too. When I was new and hearty, I was bought at a shop in the next village, and brought to this house, where I have worked for the family ever since, now boiling the water for their coffee, now making a fine hasty-pudding, and now as nice a soup, with meat-joints, carrots, turnips, and onions, as most people care about eating.

"There was a fair young bride standing upon this hearth the night I was first hung up here, (how long ago that seems!) in a white dress, with roses in her pretty, braided hair. She looked a trifle sad, — perhaps she was thinking of the dear home she had left, — so I just winked at her, and boiled merrily to show her what good friends we should become. At this she smiled pleasantly, and we were good friends ever after, for I never burned any thing to vex her, and she never upset me on the ground, so we got along very well indeed. As the years went by, there were other faces gathered about the fire, fresh and rosy children, with their games and books, or clustered about the mother's knee listening while she told a story.

"One of these was always seated here, even while the others romped in the hay-fields, and chased butterflies through the hedges, because this little one was blind. He would sit here quite silent for hours alone very patiently, for his mother had many household cares besides him. I knew that the time must be dull for the child, because he could never see the beautiful sunlight in which his brothers and sisters played, so I tried to amuse him by my own music. He seemed always pleased when I sang to him, and I used my voice so much that it is only a wonder I did not spoil it entirely. If they asked him why he smiled, he would answer, ' The kettle is talking to me.'

" The little blind child is dead now. God took him a long time ago to be a bright angel in heaven, where the wonders of that kingdom would be opened to his sight, and where he would play a golden harp in praise. The mother who stood here in her bridal dress of white is very old — so old that she never even totters to the hearth to warm her shrivelled hands at the blaze, as she used. She will go to join her little blind child soon. The brothers and sisters are men and women grown ; some have gone over the seas, and some are in great towns, but I never expect to see them again.

" I remember your interesting family very well,
my dear Cricket, although I do not recall the
particular manner in which you stared at the firelight, as there were so many of you bustling
about ; and, besides, my ideas are not so clear as
they once were, owing to the smoke of years
thickening upon my sides, and making me rather
stupid, I am afraid. Really, what a yarn I am
spinning about nothing! Pray do excuse me, it
is an infirmity of age to talk so much, although I
confess I always did enjoy it if I could find any
one to listen to me. When I commenced, I in-
tended reading the Saucepan a lecture upon
discontent and impatience, but the Cricket has
proved, better than I can hope to, that we are all
in the right place, yes, even here on this hearth-
stone, now. Keep cool, my good Saucepan, I beg
of you, — it is so much trouble, and makes one
so uncomfortable to be out of temper. Just follow my example as far as you can, even though I
have not your fine sense of right and wrong, even
though I do not know when I am imposed upon
as well as you do. At all events, I am perfectly
contented, and it will do no harm for any one to

follow my example in that, though I am but a black Kettle. Ha, ha!" laughed the Kettle gayly. "I would not change places with a king on his throne, for he has plenty of thorns in his pillow, even if it is made of satin, and I have never a care in the world, except whether I shall have to cook much or little to-morrow. .

"I had a great deal to say at my tongue's end when I started, but now I cannot find it amounts to much after all. However, comrades, have courage over small trials, never get into a pet at any thing, and help others all you can. There is a good maxim for you. That is what I have said," concluded the Kettle, his broad, old face all aglow with good-humor and kindness.

"I ask your pardon, too, Kettle," said the Saucepan, who, like all hot-tempered people, had cooled as suddenly as it had got into a passion. "I did not before consider you so much of a philosopher."

"Your life has been quiet, but the history is interesting," said the Teapot, with a patronizing air, and also some impatience, for it longed to speak itself.

"I am delighted to hear that you knew my departed parents," said the Cricket, wiping away a tear with one of his feelers. "Could you tell me, were my brothers more dutiful to them than I have been?"

"Truly," replied the Kettle, after a moment's reflection. "I now remember that your youngest sister had a disappointment in love, and remained an old maid to the day of her death. She took excellent care of your father and mother when they were old, so do not worry over that."

WHAT THE TEAPOT TOLD.

"IF you will allow me," began the Teapot, speaking very much through its nose, "I will now take my turn, as you, Grandfather Kettle, have given us some good advice; you, friend Cricket, expressed your thoughts in excellent language; and you, Miss Saucepan, have undertaken to attack us all, in what I should call a very impudent manner ——."

"There, there," interrupted the Kettle soothingly, fearing an outbreak between the two. "Let the Saucepan's temper rest for the time, and continue your story."

"Well," resumed the Teapot in a milder tone. "I was born a very great distance from here. I am a foreigner among you all, for I am a Chinese. I first saw the light of day in a large manufactory of Singapore, where workmen just like these

curious little figures painted upon my sides, with
long, narrow eyes, and hair braided in tails down
their backs, were fashioning every kind of ware,
for the Chinese are clever in all arts, and are only
equalled by their neighbors, the Japanese. I, myself, am in favor of high birth and breeding, I
confess, and I never can be mistaken for a ple-
beian as long as a remnant of my fine porcelain
body remains. That is one comfort.

"It is a satisfaction to feel that one originated
in so elegant a birthplace as I did, where an
artisan here carved a tiny group of figures upon
an ivory nut, another there traced delicate flowers
and birds upon china as frail as an egg-shell,
while a third secured a grinning idol in its shrine.
When I was completed, I flatter myself I was as
handsome a Teapot as is often seen. My lid,
which is now lost, was ornamented by a wonderful
blue dragon, with golden claws and wings spread,
and a red tail; my figure was slender and graceful; and my complexion had the most beautiful
pink tinge, which is now, unhappily, quite cooked
out of me.

"It is such a satisfaction," simpered the Teapot, with an affected air, " to feel that one has been pretty when young, although, as I have said, no one would take me for a common person, and that I was handsome there can be no doubt, from the admiration I excited when first I came to this country. But beauty must fade, sooner or later!

" After I was made, I started on a voyage almost immediately; and, although I was a long time at sea, I enjoyed myself very much. I was carefully packed in a wooden case, so that I could not move. It was rather tiresome, I ac- knowledge, never to turn an inch all the way from China to America, but then it was a nice cosy bed after all, and the wrappings about me reminded me all the time of my native land by their peculiar scent. I was not alone, I had the best of company all the way. A finely polished lacquer tray was wedged in beside me, and a more amiable traveller I never saw in my life, for he uttered no word of complaint at being obliged to stand on his head the whole time, and was ever ready for a pleasant chat. Below me in the box were a number of cups and saucers, which, as they were very much bundled up, could do very little else but sleep, while nearer to me was a wonderful enamelled turtle, within a glass dome, who was placed upon wires in such a manner as to vibrate with every jar or movement. The poor turtle grew a trifle irritable after a time, for he never ceased shaking while on board ship, and so could have no rest like the others.

"At last we entered a great harbor, where there were endless numbers of masts all interlaced at the wharves, spreading like a fine network before the city spires and roofs, and busy, puffing little steam-tugs snorted about, towing huge ships, like ants under heavy burthens.

"We were taken to a large warehouse, already crowded with beautiful things, and in the midst, upon a marble counter, the lacquer tray was placed, the teacups and myself put upon it, while the turtle stood at our side; so we made a little Chinese set all by ourselves, and felt very select indeed. When I looked at my neighbors, I felt rather disturbed in my vanity (I was very vain), still we decided to assume a very superior air, as we had come from so long a distance. At this they would all laugh, which naturally made us indignant.

"I remember particularly a gilt clock from Geneva, which had a tree with birds upon the branches, under a glass cover. This clock laughed the loudest of all at our pretensions, as it termed our disdainful airs. It would then strike a succession of soft chimes, when a music-box began to play sweetly, the birds hopped from bough to bough, twittering their own songs, and a monkey, seated beneath the tree, wagged his head at them.

"'There,' the clock would exclaim. 'Can you do better than that, my Chinese friends?' Then all the bronze statues, marble urns, glass vases, and jewel-boxes would join in a chorus of ridicule they called their sneers, but it was in reality envy, I know. We had to bear with these disagreeable creatures for so long a time, that we lost our spirits,—the tray's shining surface grew dull with melancholy, and I alone kept up to the last. 'Be of good courage; our time will come yet,' I said, in our own language, which none of the others could understand, except a box of ebony from India, who had travelled in our land. And sure enough it did come, sooner than could have been hoped. One morning a shopman appeared, followed by a gentleman in a brown wig and spectacles.

" 'Now, sir, here is as fine a clock as you will find in the city,' began the shopman, directing his customer's attention to the gilt clock, who immediately began to show itself off, with its tunes, and birds, and chimes, like the silly thing it was.

" 'Pooh!' snapped the gentleman. 'I would not have such a noisy piece in the house. It would make me crazy in five minutes.'

" The clock remained sulky and silent after this rebuff.

" 'Vases?' continued the fussy gentleman; 'no, indeed, I have so many now I should like to throw them all out the window. Statues? my house is so full of them that there is no room for me. What have we here! Chinese tea-service,—eh! That is a beautiful teapot, the finest thing you have here. I will take them all.'

" Oh, the glory of that moment! I wonder my lid had not popped off in my excitement. We

were taken up and borne away from our spiteful
associates, who stared after us as though they
would have enjoyed giving us a crack or so, by
way of a pleasant parting. We went to a fine
mansion, and any one would certainly have considered it no wonder that the fussy gentleman
should have wanted no more clocks or vases, for
he had enough already to stock a bazaar. Two
figures of nymphs at the entrance held up shells
filled with trailing vines and mosses. A group
of water-spirits supported an aquarium in the
window recess, where the slanting sunbeams fell
upon darting fish, brilliant-colored marine worms,
and green, waving seaweeds. At the curve of the
broad stairway was stationed the goddess Diana,
with her bow strung and a hind crouching at her
feet, while from every niche peeped little forms,
here a fairy in a half-opened rose, there a bird
hovering over its nest.

"I could see no more, for I was taken up stairs
at once. We were placed upon a cabinet in a
small room, where the firelight flickered upon the
walls, all hung with heavy folds of damask, and a
little dog, like a mop of white wool, lay coiled up

into a ball upon the hearth-rug, fast asleep. I have good reason to remember 'Tiny,' as he was called, for, had it not been for him, I might now be still in that beautiful home, instead of a farmer's kitchen.

"Ugh!" cried the Teapot, with disgust.

"The next day our duties began by a smart lady's-maid arranging us upon a table, with a dainty breakfast, and filling me, for the first time, with a drawing of tea. Then she opened the door of another room, and wheeled a lady to the fireside. I can see this lady's pale face even now; she was dressed in black, with a white cap upon her gray hair; she never smiled, and seldom spoke. The fussy gentleman would bustle in to pay her a call, another grave lady, and even rosy, merry children, but it never seemed to me that her face changed at all; she would just sit looking at the fire until night came, when they would wheel her back to her room again.

"It was such a pleasant, quiet life we led there, with nothing much to do but minister to the wants of the invalid lady, then talk together about our own affairs, in our shady corner, where the perfume of sweet flowers floated about us. But, alas, it could not last always! One night the maid omitted to clear the table, and went off to gossip instead. Master Tiny, by ill-luck, must needs wake up just then, yawn, stretch himself, and begin to sniff about him. He was not long in discovering there was a morsel of something good left upon the supper-tray, so he leaped up into a chair, put his paws upon the edge of the table in hopes of reaching the coveted meat, when he lost his balance, fell, and brought the whole thing down to the floor with him, scattering dishes right and left. When he found what a crash he had made, he was frightened, and crawled away under the sofa, where he sat, with his small nose poked out, to see what would come of it all. The lady's-maid found a cup shivered to fragments, and my beautiful spout broken off.

"This comes of having lap-dogs where fine china is kept. Of course I was only considered a disgrace after that, so I had to bid the dear tray and turtle good-by, and left them in their fine home, where they doubtless are now. I went down to the kitchen and was given to the cook, who kept tobacco in me, and hid me away in the cellar, where she used to go privately and smoke a pipe; then she told fibs, and said the smoke came from the wood-sawyer.

"Imagine the humiliation of my descent in life, living in the same house with my relatives whom I could never see, for how can a teapot walk up stairs?

"I sat neglected upon an old shelf, as the cook was dismissed suddenly; and the spiders spun cob-webs all over me, as if to show their contempt for my humbled condition. At last the smart lady's-maid came mincing down cellar one day for a particular bottle of wine, with her fresh dress held up in one hand, and a candle in the other. She discovered me, and, taking me down, dusted me with her apron.

"'Dear, dear,' she said, 'how dirty you are by this time, that sat so dacent up stairs!'

"She carried me out of the cellar, which was a relief at the time, for I longed for a breath of fresh air and a sight of the sun once more; but I should not care now if she had left me there for ever. She set me down in the kitchen, and

went away again. I was hustled and knocked
about here for a time, in every one's way, then a
little beggar-girl stole me, and hid me in her basket. She played with me for a while, then threw
me aside upon a dust-mound.

" By daylight next morning a curious old man,
with long white hair, a queer cap upon his head,
a bag over his shoulder, and an iron prong in his
hand, came prowling along. He probed the
mound with the prong, picked out rags, bits of
paper, and me, whom he tossed into the bag with
the rest. This old man was a miser. He lived
in a dark, gloomy old house, where he hoarded
up his wealth, and almost starved himself to
death. So fearful was he of being robbed of his
gold, that he lived alone with an old cat, and
spent his time toiling about the streets as an
humble rag-picker. When he reached home, he
carefully locked the door, then began sifting the
contents of his bag. I had supposed he could
have nothing but rubbish, when, to my surprise, I
saw him sort out a lace veil, a diamond bracelet,
a kid glove, and other articles lost in the streets
the previous night. I wondered what use he

would put me to, and soon found out. First he gave me a bath, which I needed badly enough, then he placed in me the diamond bracelet, and from an old leather bag filled me up with broad gold pieces.

" A costly filling for a teapot, you will say, and I agree to that, but the gold felt cold in comparison to nice oolong tea. I was then put into a chest and locked up, in company with a large, iron-bound box. It was a dull life, for the strong box was not a lively companion, and I grew heartily tired of the miser gloating over me, and chinking my contents.

" One night two thieves softly cut the pane of glass near the fastening of the window, slid it open, and entered the room. The miser in his bed of rags appeared to sleep soundly, so they forced the fastening of the chest where I was concealed, and, having examined my contents, tried to lift the heavy box as well. They were startled by a sudden shout ; the miser, who had feigned sleep for fear they would kill him, had stolen to another window, alarmed the watch, and fired his pistol. One thief grasped me, jumped from the

window to a low roof, and made away as fast as
he could, leaving the other to follow. He went
on rapidly, under shadow of the walls, until
he reached the city limits, and so out into the
open country. He walked, it seemed to me, miles
by the highway, before he paused at a small hovel
and knocked. The door was opened, but he
stopped to empty the bracelet and gold into his
hand and toss me away before entering.

"It is only a wonder I did not crash to fragments, and so make an end of it,—but no! I
landed in a soft place, and so remained whole.
I lay there a long time, looking up at the clear
sky, listening to the wind rustling through the
ripening grain-fields, and not caring much what
came next.

"A farmer with some bleating little lambs in
his cart drove along one day, and, attracted by
my unusual appearance, he took me up, but, not
liking me much afterward, tossed me back beside the lambs, who bleated in my ears until
I was deafened by their noise. He drove into
this very barnyard, so I am near the close of my
history, you perceive, and the man-servant Zede-

kiah took a fancy to me, so the farmer gave me
to him. He smartened me up with soap and
water, then presented me to Hulda, whom he is
making love to, as any of you may have seen with
half an eye before this.

"Life has been a sad disappointment to me,
perhaps because in my conceit I wished to be
esteemed above all others. That is what I have
told," said the Teapot with a melancholy sigh.

"No wonder you feel a difference from high
society to us," said the good old Kettle.

"I should liked to have visited your native
land," said the Cricket reflectively.

"I beg your pardon, too, dear Madame Teapot," apologized the Saucepan, touched by the
Teapot's misfortunes. "I now find that my ill-
temper has brought much good, and, since it has
led to the recital of your histories, I do not regret
that I boiled over."

"As we have enjoyed this evening so much, I
have a proposal to make ; however, as I hear some
one coming, I will wait until another time," said
the Cricket.

He had scarcely ceased speaking, when Hulda

bustled in from the dairy, and Zedekiah from the barn. The Cricket retired to his mansion behind a brick, the Kettle still sang, but the Saucepan and Teapot were as still as if they never had spoken in their lives.

The next night they were all very curious to hear what the Cricket had to say. Their impatience was the greater, that he did not appear for a long time. Finally he trotted in through the crack, with a very important, business-like air. " Excuse me for being so late," he said, seating himself. " I have been in the town library all day, trying to learn something from my relatives there. Now I will tell you my plan. Supposing that we form a club, just like the gentlemen in cities. We then can find a story to tell in our circle every night."

" That will be delightful," exclaimed the Teapot. " I now remember the fussy gentleman, with the brown wig, belonged to the ' Century,' or yearly, or something of that sort."

" I never heard of such a thing, but I dare say it is nice," said the Kettle.

" Well then, if you will allow me, I will arrange

it," began the Cricket, with a modest air, "for when I lived in the lawyer's window I heard a great deal about such things. We must have a president, a chairman, and a committee. Now I propose that the Kettle is president, the Teapot chairman —"

"No, no!" cried the Teapot and Saucepan, together, "you shall be chairman."

So it was arranged, and the Kettle felt very grand, indeed, with his new title of president.

"We must all be thinking of something to tell, and to-morrow shall be your turn, friend Kettle," advised the Cricket.

The next night the Kettle Club met, and prepared to enter upon their duties. The Cricket had on a fresh suit of clothes, in honor of the occasion; the Saucepan's sides had been rubbed until they reflected the firelight; and the Teapot really looked handsome, for all it had no nose but a broken one.

"I have been thinking all day of a story that I heard the young mother tell her little blind child," said the Kettle, and began : —

OSMUNDA AND THE FAIRIES

THE LITTLE MAIDEN OSMUNDA.

———◆———

"MANY hundred years ago there lived at Loch Tyne a worthy waterman. His home was very small and poor, his wife dead, yet his hearth owned what he would not have exchanged for all the world beside, in his daughter Osmunda.

" All day she took care of their humble cottage, singing at her work, and then at eventide she might be found on the shore watching for the flash of the ferryman's oars over the blue waters ; while to him the small figure with blooming cheek and golden hair seemed more beautiful than an angel.

" One night, when the two were partaking of their frugal meal, a fugitive rushed in with a pale face and streaming hair. He told them, in gasping breaths of terror, that a troop of Danes were on the march to the ferry, and would soon arrive. Then the fugitive rushed on again, to hide anywhere from the cruel foe, leaving the ferryman speechless with sudden dread.

" Soon there sounded over the hillside a distant bugle note, that rang out upon the air, and seemed to startle even the insects, humming in the sunbeams. At this sound the ferryman took his daughter to the boat, and rowed out upon the Loch. They landed at an island, where the father, with a prayer for her safety, left Osmunda, and returned with all speed to the shore. He had scarcely done so, when the enemy arrived, all clad in steel armor, with fierce eyes and yellow beards. They did not harm the ferryman, but bade him carry them across the Loch without delay.

" Little Osmunda, left all alone, crouched under the shadow of the ferns and began to cry, for she was afraid the fierce soldiers would kill her father and burn his home. A rustling sounded among the leaves, like the patter of raindrops, and Osmunda fancied she heard her name repeated in all directions. She looked about her half fearfully and noticed one fern more gracefully beautiful than the rest, upon which perched a number of elves dressed in green; then the trunk opened, and the Fairy of the island advanced with her train.

"She poised herself lightly upon a lily-leaf, near the astonished Osmunda, who could not but admire the Fairy's slippers, which were made of cowslips, embroidered with drops of dew. 'Welcome to my island!' said the Fairy, with a voice like crystal bells.

"Then Osmunda thanked her with a courtesy, for she had a great respect for fairies, as, indeed, should every good little boy and girl.

"The good Fairy waved her sceptre, which was a tiny spray of smoke-tree, tipped with gold, and all her subjects set about various pursuits for the entertainment of their guest. One group of sprites, who were evidently skilful cooks, to judge from their French caps, made of spider's web, with aprons to match, began to compound wonderful dishes in flower-cups and upon pebble platters. Another set commenced to weave blades of grass into a dining table, and all the while the good Fairy sat poised upon her lily-leaf giving orders, and smiling upon little Osmunda, who felt very happy indeed.

" Suddenly there came a pause in the preparations, — the cooks whisked off their aprons, and armed themselves with thorn-spikes, the good Fairy leaped from her perch to vanish into the palace of the fern-tree, and presently re-appeared all clad in armor of chestnut-burs, which would certainly seem invulnerable ; then, assembling her forces, she marched to the shore, a band of locusts and grasshoppers sounding martial music the while.

" Now the cause of this disturbance was a wicked Fairy, who lived on another island, and who had been filled with rage, that the ferryman should not have brought his daughter to her dominions, that the little girl might have been frightened to death by lizards, and toads, and rats. As this pleasure had been denied her, the wicked Fairy had still determined to do what mischief she could ; so entering her chariot, which was a thistle, drawn by three water-snakes, and attended by frogs, and a host of buzzing, stinging gnats and mosquitos, she now appeared.

"Osmunda peeped through the leaves, and thought the wicked Fairy a very ugly little old woman, for she was not only dressed in the wings of the dragon-fly, with two horns upon her head, but she wore a pair of blue spectacles upon her sharp nose.

"'Ho, ho!' cried the wicked Fairy, shaking her fist. 'Give me the ferryman's daughter, or I will show the Danes where she is.'

"As her threat had no effect upon the minute warriors that lined the shore, she waved her wand, and lo! the most beautiful lights, of red, blue, and green, darted about the island, shooting out stars in every direction, and twining into rings of flame.

The Danes, crossing the water in the evening shadows, saw the many-colored flashes, and shouted aloud their astonishment, while the heart of the ferryman sank with fear. The captain ordered him to steer toward the island, but, ere they reached it, the Kelpies, whose home is at the bottom of the lake, came to the surface, and quenched the fire by the spray from water-reeds.

" So the Norsemen turned away again, thinking that surely they had reached a strange land.

" Then the wicked Fairy scowled with disappointment, and all her army hissed with spite, because the grasshopper band of the good Fairy scraped their legs and wings in defiant music. Finally the invader sent back to her home two trusty mosquito messengers, who speedily returned with a dozen ugly serpents, that set to work upon the roots of the ferns with their sharp fangs, and pierced them through until they fell over into the water, leaving the little maiden Osmunda wholly exposed to the view of the cruel soldiers in her father's boat. Nay, to make her the plainer visible, wicked elves fluttered up above her, and held conch-shells, all lined with a glow like sunshine, which reflected upon Osmunda's fair head, and surrounded her like a glory.

" And over the water the Danes saw her with wonder, while the ferryman's arms drooped to his side, for he thought all lost.

" Then the good Fairy floated out upon the waves, and spread out her wings, which grew larger and larger until they obscured every thing from view, in a white mist. Several other attempts did the wicked Fairy make, but her adversary remained a veil which human eyes could not penetrate. With a great deal of hubbub among her followers, croaking and sputtering, she went back to her home, baffled and chagrined.

" Osmunda had watched all these proceedings, first with fear, then joy when her fairies gained the day. She now began to wonder what would be done next, as the beautiful ferns were pierced and broken by the cruel serpent-stings. She had not thought of this long, when she beheld one of the warriors approach a toadstool, and tap upon it with his spear. It opened and out popped a manikin of solemn visage, who carried an acorn under his arm. He was evidently a physician of no mean repute, and the acorn proved to be a medicine-chest, from which he took a certain infallible balm and plasters. These the fairies used to mend the broken ferns, and with such good success that the stems soon became erect again.

" After which the manikin doctor entered his toadstool mansion again.

3*

" Then what a happy place was the island!

" As it was already dark, the sprites hung glow-worm lanterns on all the branches, and made such a feast that Osmunda wished there might be nothing to eat in all the world but sugar-candy. The grasshoppers scraped away on their fiddles, and the fairies danced in the twinkling light, until Osmunda's eyelids grew heavy with so many marvels, and she fell asleep. Instantly the good Fairy commanded silence, and ordered her couch of rose-leaves spread near her little visitor; while some of the Royal Body Guard nestled among Osmunda's curls to make her dreams pleasant.

" When morning dawned, the ferryman ventured in search of his child, whom he found fast asleep upon the moss, still dreaming of the fairies, that had all vanished. Then the ferryman knelt down and uttered a prayer of gratitude for her preservation, and, placing her in the boat, returned home. But although she grew to womanhood on the distant shore, she never ceased to visit the Island of Royal Ferns, which bears her name, Osmunda, to this day."

When the Kettle had finished his story, he drew a long breath of satisfaction.

" I was afraid I should get it all wrong," said
he, " for it is a very long time since I heard it, and
I have no very good memory. Now, had I made
a mistake, and had the wicked Fairy carry off
Osmunda, it would have been sad."

" Dreadful !" exclaimed the Saucepan.

" If it was not too late, I would tell my story
this moment, as it is on the very tip of my
tongue," said the Cricket, skipping out into the
room to look at the clock. " Oh, dear me, yes,
you would all fall asleep before I had half done,
so we will wait."

However, the Cricket's turn did arrive, and he
began briskly.

THE ADVENTURES OF A BOTTLE.

—◆—

"NOW in giving my life (this is the way the bottle told its story), I know very well that I have not had a more adventurous history than many of my brothers; for how can you tell, pray, where the wine-bottles in your cellar, or the medicine vials upon the mantel-piece, have been before you ever saw them? still, as a good friend of mine has promised to write my story, I shall just give it to you as it comes into my head, or cork rather, for I suppose a bottle really has no head, for I am very old now, and my thoughts may wander a trifle.

"Well, I was born in a great, glowing, hot furnace, where I was a mere bubble of confined air on the end of a long iron tube which a man held and blew through until he was red in the face.

with puffing cheeks, and I had become quite fat
with his blowing. I felt very limp and weak in
the roaring fire, and really did not care much
whether I melted altogether or not. However,
after being carried through the cooler air and
popped into a mould where I was allowed to settle a bit, I felt more comfortable ; for my sides
began to harden and my neck to form. They
did not allow me to rest long, though, you may
be sure ; for I had hardly time to shape myself
before I was whisked out again, scraped, polished, and tumbled about until I was tired of the
whole business of being made. At last, I was
finished, and packed into a basket with others of
my age, and we were rattled off over rough pav-
ing stones, in a smart wagon, to a large building
where we were hurried into a cellar, and plunged
into a great tank of cold water before we could
catch our breaths.

"Well, well, I cannot pretend to say how the
others felt, although I remember they made a
great gurgling and sputtering, for I was too
much occupied with myself to notice them. All
I know is that, with ideas entirely confused, I

was first filled up with water; then stood upon my head to drain until I thought I should be crazed. I dare say you suppose that a bottle can never have a headache, or a pain in its stomach; but perhaps, if you had been only just born in a hot furnace, you would not have relished a cold bath any better than I did.

"Afterward I was filled with excellent wine, a cork driven tight in my throat, and I was placed on a shelf. I must have remained there for several years; and do not suppose that one cannot learn wisdom in the world's ways even on the shelf of a dark cellar. There was a very old and wise bottle on the opposite side of the place, who was fond of exhorting us younger ones about our follies, and also liked to tell us of what he had seen in his day. When we were not listening to him, we dozed off pleasantly in our several corners. At last this quiet life was broken. It must have been about Christmas time, I think, for I know our cellar had grown very cold, and the wine danced within us, as if longing to be drank, when some men came in and began to take down some of us. I wondered if I should go too; and, yes, I was taken from where I had stood so long, to go out into the world again. I went to a very grand house this time, and was placed in a tin case on ice, which was very good for the wine, no doubt, but it gave me a bad cold. So it is; *we* are never regarded, only what is inside of us. Well, at last I was lifted from the ice-box, wiped upon a napkin, and taken to the dining-room by a waiter in a white jacket.

"I had never seen a gaslight in all my life, and it now flickered and flashed about me until I fairly winked and blinked. However, when I recovered myself, I found I was upon a carved sideboard that supported brilliant, polished silver ware; large urns of graceful shape, and broad shining salvers which reflected gay colors, people, and the painted walls upon their smooth surface. I felt delighted with the change from a musty old cellar to this fresh, wonderful scene, and only hoped that the guests at table might not be thirsty enough to want me for a long time, so that I might see them all.

"At the head of the table sat a very small, fat

gentleman behind a large turkey, so large, indeed, that I could only see the tip of his nose, which seemed to me a pity, as he was all the time trying to peep over the barrier; although his guests seemed to think to like the turkey the best of the two. Then there was a tall lady in a green satin dress, who looked very cross when the waiter slipped and poured gravy down her back (as well she might), and another lady who pecked at her food like a bird, and tossed her head very much, and a gentleman in spectacles that ate nothing but pickles. I could see no more for the wine began to bubble inside of me; the waiter caught me up in a hurry, cut the wires which held my cork,—when puff! bang! away it shot straight into the eye of the gentleman with spectacles, who certainly partook of no more pickles for that night.

"Ah me! how the sparkling wine poured out of my throat, leaving me empty and miserable!

"No one valued me any more, so I was thrust out into a dark passage where I lay neglected until I was thrown upon a heap of rubbish, and the rain fell upon me and the cold nights coated my sides with ice. At last a boy came whistling by, and, stooping, suddenly caught me up, gave me a toss in the air, tucked me under his arm, and walked away. He went by many handsome streets, darted round this corner, turned up that alley, and finally paused before a small shop which he entered. It was a dark, close place, I noticed as we passed through, with jars of candy, a few shrivelled apples and oranges, some wooden chairs, and old clothes. The boy pushed aside a cloak which served as a curtain before a door, and entered a back room where an old woman was cooking in a saucepan over the fire.

" ' What have you got there, Dick ? ' " she inquired, as he placed me upon the window-seat.

" ' A bottle to put some tadpoles in, to see their legs grow.'

" Nothing more was said, and I was left undisturbed while the old lady spread the table for supper. She had no sooner made these preparations than a young man and woman came in to join the other two at the meal. A right snug little party they made of it, and I dare say I should have enjoyed it with them had I not been a bottle. The young man was a sailor, and would go on board his ship that very night, and the girl seemed very sorry about his leaving. When supper was finished, the two young people made a pretence of going into the shop for some-. thing, and I saw the sailor steal a kiss from his sweetheart, quite plain, for a bottle may have its wits about it surely.

" Well, after that, the old woman and girl began to pack the sailor's chest. They folded his clothes neatly, and the girl put a new Bible in one side for a present, and the old woman added a blue pocket-handkerchief; then they began to consider medicines. The grandmother must put up a little spiced brandy for colic, — only what should she pour it into? — why, me, of course. I was filled, corked, and laid beside a flannel shirt in the chest.

" Well, thought I, what next?

" We started on the voyage. I rolled and lurched about with every motion of the ship in a very uncomfortable manner, although I was not at all sea-sick. The sailor one day unlocked the chest, and, in removing some clothes, took me out. I saw him look at the Bible, and a tear fell upon it when he opened the leaves. The cordial within me was soon disposed of; for it was so good that all the crew were taken so ill, as soon as they had tasted it, that they had to have more. I was knocked about anywhere after that, and it is only a wonder I did not roll overboard. We had been to sea a long, long time, when the air became quite still under the hot sun, and the sea as smooth as glass. The captain paced the deck, and looked about him very anxiously; but for days the sky looked like a brazen dome, and the sea glittered without a wave.

" One night a dark line of cloud grew in the east, and spread up the heavens: the sea began to heave, the wind to whistle, until the rain poured in torrents mingling with the foam, and we rushed through the darkness like a bird. Oh, what a time that was! The lightning flashed about us, and great water-spouts began to rear themselves in spinning columns from sea to sky.

" The young sailor wrote on a slip of paper with

a pencil, put it into me, and corked me tight. Just then the vessel gave a fearful plunge, a great wave foamed up, she struggled a moment with her masts bent like whips, then went down!

" When the next morning's sun rose there was not a soul of them all alive, not a remnant of the cargo left; only a little bottle bobbing up and down on the waves. It was not so bad for a time, floating over the broad ocean with nothing to be seen night or day but an occasional fish leaping up; but then it becomes tedious, and one longs for the sight of a brother bottle. At last, one morning I saw land to my great joy. While the current bore me swiftly toward it, a large, white shark came gliding along, opened wide his jaws armed with sharp teeth, and swallowed me whole.

" Well, thought I, lying in the shark's stomach, what next? His sharkship did not feel very well after eating so strange a morsel. He tried to make me digest, but I would not; so he was glad to eject me again. When I bobbed up in the sea once more, the land was gone! I gave up all hope of being any thing but a sailor all my life, when one day I espied a stately ship sweeping toward me. Ah! sighed I, they will never notice poor me. They did, however, for they mistook my black body for a man's head, sent a boat to me, and discovered the error. However, they carried me on board, for the captain and all of them tried to read my paper, but could not because it was written in a different language.

"They took me to the port where they were bound, and the captain presented me to his uncle, for him to read the words of the poor young sailor. Now this uncle was a very wise person in all sciences, and I was taken to his laboratory, where he was then engaged in planning a flying machine. The captain sailed away again, and I remained in the corner; for the wise gentleman had quite forgotten me, so interested was he in his flying machine. One day he finished this work, and determined to make an ascent through the air as an aëronaut does in the balloon. While preparing to start, he took me up without noticing the paper inside me, and filled me with some chemical that he required. The machine was not like any thing ever seen before, for it was not a balloon, a boat, or any other conveyance. It must have looked like some strange monster as it rose slowly in the air and floated over a large city. The people rushed out upon the roofs, and paused in the streets to watch us in amazement. Up we went through the air, above the clouds, higher and higher, until it would seem that we must be near the moon itself, when a curious, hissing noise issued from a pipe beside me; the wise gentleman tried, in alarm, to remedy the trouble, but it was too late; there was a sudden rush, a volume of smoke, a bright flame, and I was spinning through the air down toward the earth again. Well, thought I, if I reach the ground without having all my bones broken, it will be lucky. The wind caught me in eddies, and whirled me about in the clouds, yet down I went faster and faster, when, with a crash, I reached the ground. I must have fainted away there; for I see no reason why a bottle should not do so on occasion, particularly when its neck is broken, and only a remnant of its body left.

"When I recovered, I was lying beside a river

where the grass and buttercups grew, and the water rippled over the pebbles with a pleasant sound. Near by, I noticed a large, old house with many gables and chimneys, from which some children came running down the bank to play. In their frolic, they found a little, green frog, which skipped away nimbly, but one of them caught it in his hand.

"'We will take him home in this broken bottle,' cried the child. I recognized the language they spoke, and knew that I must be in my native land again. They placed the frog in my broken remains, put a handkerchief over the top, and went back to the house, where they mounted to the attic, that they might enjoy a dog's pranks with their little captive.

"I have never left this attic since. Here my wanderings ceased; for a young maid used to come up here when her household labor was done, and sit by the window with her wheel to spin flax; and one day, an owl, disturbed from its nest, came fluttering against the window, and broke a pane of glass with his heavy wings. Then the maid looked about for some ready means of mending it, to keep out the cold wind, and she discovered me where I had been left by the children. She fitted me into the hole in the window-pane, and I have been there ever since.

"Many years have passed away, for a bottle is long-lived, you know. The maid that used to spin here is an old woman; the children that caught the little green frog are all dead; nobody lives in this great, old house but the bats and I.

"People have a foolish fancy, that, because the place is old and deserted, it is haunted by ghosts and evil spirits; they even say there is a strange sound, like voices, in the attic at night; but that is only the wind sighing through the window-pane by me. These are some of my adventures, which my kind friend has promised to write for me, — it is only the life of a bottle, after all."

The Cricket ceased speaking; the Saucepan and Teapot nodded their approbation with beaming looks, but the Kettle was silent.

"Where did you hear this story?" questioned the Saucepan.

"When I was living in town, I was strolling over a great house one evening, and heard a nursery-maid reading it to the children; so I just crept under the fender to listen too." All this time the Kettle hung motionless, without a sign of life.

The Saucepan and Teapot whispered together over what was best to be done under the circumstances, and the Cricket grew very red in the face with offended pride.

"Well," said he, at length, leaping up in a pet, and buttoning his coat, "I have seen better manners."

"My dear Cricket," interposed the Teapot coaxingly, "do wait a moment," for he was making off as fast as his legs would carry him.

"Kettle, what do you think of the story?"

Alas! the Kettle only answered by a snore.

Then it was that the Club had nearly dissolved. The Cricket was in hot wrath that his story should not have been better appreciated than to have the president fall asleep in the midst; while the committee did not know how to pacify the irate chairman.

"You know that the Kettle is really very old," whispered the Saucepan.

"Eh!" cried the Kettle, suddenly waking up. "What do you say down there?"

"We were saying that we had better not have any more evening stories, if we cannot keep awake," said the Cricket, with great dignity. He then, with a bow, retired to his house. Oh, what a scolding the committee gave the poor Kettle, although he was a president, for spoiling every thing in this way!

"Pooh!" he said pettishly, "I was not asleep: I was only reflecting. However, I will beg the Cricket's forgiveness." How were they to present an apology to the injured chairman, when none of them could reach the Cricket, and he would not come out? Finally, an ant went trotting by, and they all called upon him eagerly, to stop.

"I am very busy," said the ant, halting. "Speak, and be quick about it." So they told him they wanted him to deliver the apology to the Cricket.

"He may eat me up, while I am doing it," said the ant, rubbing his right ear; "but if you will tell me where I can find a lump of sugar afterward, Teapot, I will risk it."

Next evening, the Cricket appeared quite molli-
fied by the apology, and the Club met as usual.

It was now the Teapot's turn, who decided to
relate a story which the Geneva clock had told,
when they all lived together in the warehouse.

It was : —

OLÈ, THE DISCONTENTED.

"THERE once lived on the bleak, rugged coast of Norway a worthy fisherman by the name Claës, who was respected by all the village for his kind heart and honesty. The fisherman, like almost all his neighbors, was very poor, and could hardly sustain his large family by his scanty earnings.

"Among his children was a stranger whom Dame Katrine had christened Olè, because they did not know his real name, for he had been wrecked on the shore some years before, and had since been treated as his own by the good Claës.

"Olè was not a good boy, for a silly idea had entered his head that he was superior to those about him, which naturally made him vain and proud. He fancied he was the son of some great prince or merchant over the seas, who would send for him sometime, to live in a grand castle for the rest of his life. The poor boy would pass hours thinking of the glorious time when he should wear velvet and satin; then every thing in the little hut of Claës would seem so mean and poor. The children would say, 'There comes discontented Olè, let us put on a long face like his,— so!'

"Now Olè loved Dame Katrine very much, and, hearing her express a wish for some feathers to stuff a pillow, he determined to visit a rocky island where the birds'-nests were to be found. His heart beat high, for he knew it would be very dangerous, still he was a brave lad, and longed to surprise Claës with his courage.

"When morning dawned, he crept down to the water's edge, with a rope and bag, unmoored the boat, and pushed off. He rowed out upon the smooth water which the sun just tinged with crimson from the eastern sky, to where the headland rose like a huge, black giant, with the breakers dashing and foaming about the base.

Olè was obliged to row beyond this point to the island, which lay further out to sea. Had not the boy been used to the water, he would hardly have ventured out of the sheltered harbor to where his boat was tossed like a cockle-shell upon the waves, and it required no little skill to reach the more sheltered part of the island. Having secured the boat, he leaped from it and began to scramble up the steep, slippery ascent. He climbed over one boulder here and another one there, frequently bruising both hands and feet, until he found himself at a giddy height, where he could look up at the sky, and down to the foaming ocean, into which a single false step would throw him. Olè had already made several trips to this island with Claës in search of feathers and eggs, but he had always remained in the boat. He fastened his rope to an iron bar, which was securely driven into the rock, put the other end about his waist, then, with his bag over one shoulder, swung himself down.

" ' Now if the prince, my father, could see me, he would be proud ; ' he cried, and the wind and sea laughed together over it.

"He found it no easy matter to reach some ledges, as he was so small, besides the nests were empty and deserted in many places, so that he was discouraged, and would have returned home had he not been ashamed to. Finally he discovered, to his great joy, two nests with the beautiful eggs warmly hidden in the soft lining. Olè did not stop to think how cruel it was to thus rob the poor birds, but, eagerly filling the bag, he swung himself back from one point to another until he arrived in safety at the iron bar.

"Soon after he was rowing off with the bag of feathers safe in the boat with him. To his surprise, he found that the sun was already sinking in the west, the wind blew roughly, and the sea was running so high that Olè's feeble attempts, for he was very tired, proved unavailing in the attempt to guide himself home. He grew frightened: what if he did not carry the feathers to Dame Katrine, after all? A great wave reared like a mountain at a distance, and came slowly sweeping toward the little boat, while Olè, gazing at it in terror, fancied he could see strange faces and forms in the green depths, until it towered up over him, and he was rushing down, down through the waters. He found himself in the most wonderful garden, the paths of which were formed of fine sand, while among the waving sea-weeds, some as large as trees, others as delicate as silky threads, beautiful flowering anemones clustered, purple, pink, and yellow-starred, and bright-colored mollusks crawled about.

" Olè noticed a cave close by, and pushed aside the curtain of moss which hung before it, to explore the place. The cave was ornamented by numerous crystals, that spread a fringe from the dome, and reflected every light like sparkling jewels, and in the blue water below sported strange forms, mermaids with green leaves twined in their long hair, and tritons with trumpets. Upon a throne of coral sat the Fairy Linia, in a robe of gold-fishes' fins, a diadem of pearls upon her head, and a sceptre of pink flowering coralline.

" ' You have come to my dominions, where you shall be well treated; but my grandfather, the great god Neptune, allows me to rule here on condition that every mortal who comes to **my** cave shall be changed for a year's time,' said the Fairy to Olè, who made a low bow. She touched him with her wand twice, and he felt a strange shiver pass over him; his feet clung together and turned into a fish-tail, and he was swimming about like his companions.

" 'It is all very fine,' thought the new fish, as he flapped his tail with a good deal of splashing about, for he did not know how to manage it very well yet, 'but what will they do at night down here?'

" He soon saw how the ocean was illuminated. The medusæ, or jelly-fish, sailed up and down, sending forth a pale, phosphorescent glow, and resembling crystal globes of light; numerous fish darted swiftly about, leaving flashes of blue and green in their path, which served to show the outline of some rock, or a huge whale's black head; and the sea-pens quivered below, emitting brilliant sparkles through the clear water.

" All the wonders of this life beneath the waves

4*

did Olè behold, yet, true to his name of the discontented, he grew tired of being a fish, of at-
tending the Fairy Linia, and of his companions,
whom he considered stupid and tiresome at the
best.   He wished he could walk upon the land
again, even see Claës and the children ; so he
decided to ask the Fairy to change him to a boy
once more.   The time he chose to speak was
when he accompanied her as a charioteer.   Her
carriage consisted of a shell lined with soft moss,
supported by dolphins, and drawn by sea-horses.
This was her barouche : when it was bad weather
she drove in her brougham, the oyster-shells
closed, or her coupé, a scallop.   She paid visits
of ceremony to her friends, the Prince of the
Sea-Mice, the Queen of the Cowries, and the
Grand-Duke of the Lobsters, all of whom were
neighbors.

" ' You wish to be a mortal again, I see,' she
said, before Olè could speak, ' but you will not
be happy then.   I will give you this crystal box,
which contains a row of turquoise beads.   You
can have ten wishes gratified by slipping a bead
from the gold cord, and tossing it toward the

sun, calling my name twice. If you break the beads, you will be punished as you deserve.'

" She then gave him the beautiful crystal box, which he had no sooner received than he rose to the surface of the sea.

" 'I am tired of all this,' he exclaimed, 'I wish I was a bird.'

" ' What bird ?' said a distant voice.

" 'Fairy Linia, Fairy Linia, I would be a parrot,' he said, tossing a bead toward the sun.

" He had scarce pronounced these words when he felt himself growing smaller and lighter, until he rose in the air on outspread wings, which were so beautiful that his own eyes were dazzled by his new magnificence. On, on he sped through the clear air so high above the earth that the town steeples looked like mere thorn-spikes, and the rivers seemed silver ribbons threading the valleys. Olè knew he was flying over hundreds of miles, yet so strong were his pinions, so delightful the great, golden sun blazing directly above him by day, and the pale, clear moon by night, that he felt no fatigue. Other birds passed him, hawks swooped down over him, and great eagles clashed their heavy wings so near that he trembled with fear that their keen, bright eyes should notice him, but he escaped all, for the crystal box, which was secured by the gold cord under one wing rendered him invisible.

"As he went further toward the south, he could feel how warm the air grew, perfumed by flowers and scented shrubs, and he finally noticed a small lake glittering far below him, in which he decided to regard himself. The sun was just setting, and all the birds and insects were awakening from their long silence of the heated noonday; gorgeous butterflies flitted about, turtle-doves of violet color cooed softly along the margin of the lake, other birds, some black as velvet, shaded with orange, some blue with tails of burnished gold, twittered in the lofty trees, among whom Olè recognized many parrots with green and red feathers, climbing the rose-acacias by means of their beaks and claws. In the clear waters of the lake abounded beautiful silver-fish with fins of purple, and blue-fish with fins of scarlet that rested almost motionless upon the surface. 'Will you allow me to see myself in the water?' said

Olè politely to a large fish, who seemed very proud of himself. The large fish laughed at this, and said,—

"'You belong to the air; the water is made for us; however, you can use this pool for a looking-glass.'

"So Olè peeped into the basin, where his whole image was reflected. His coat was of the most brilliant scarlet, his tail and wings tipped with gold, while upon his head was a crest of the same hue, which certainly gave him a very stylish appearance. While he was still admiring himself, an old gray parrot came hopping down to the shore on one leg, for he had the gout.

"'Halloo!' cried the gray parrot, cocking his head on one side.

"'Halloo!' replied Olè, his gaze still fixed on the water.

"'Pray, where did you come from, that you answer your elders in this way?' said the gray parrot, his feathers ruffling with anger.

"'I really beg your pardon, sir,' said Olé, 'but my new clothes are so handsome I cannot cease admiring them.'

"'The folly of youth,' said the gray parrot, stepping back a pace, and putting his spectacles upon his nose, the better to examine the other. 'Yes,' he added, 'you are a handsome young fellow enough, and I should judge from the cut of your knee-breeches that your tailor is a good one. Dear me, I do like to see a parrot well dressed; my coat is plain but neat, you see. I have two sons, though, that are the trial of my life, for one of them has fallen in love, and cares not a pin whether he is shabby or not, and the other is so unlucky as to get into scrapes enough. Last night he lost his tail entirely. But bless me!' he exclaimed briskly, 'I must take you home to see my wife and daughters.' So saying, he led the way to a large tree, where his family lived upon a branch.

"Olè was delighted with his new condition, for what could be better than to eat delicious fruits, and live in a grand forest, where one could see great serpents, the powerful jaguar, the swift-footed deer bounding along to the river-bed to drink, and sluggish alligators occasionally poking their ugly snouts above the bank?

"'The parrot life is what suits me best,' said Olè, 'so I shall never care to be a boy or fish again, but I will marry the gray parrot's striped daughter, and settle.'

"So he married the striped daughter, and there were great rejoicings at the wedding, for the gray parrot had feared she would be an old maid, after all. Alas! Olè did not enjoy the life of a married bird half so well as that of a bachelor, for his wife had a sharp tongue of her own, and was very fond of scolding. As his home was not happy, he went with his unlucky brother-in-law (the one who had lost his tail). This parrot was very lively and gay by nature, and, having more love for play than any kind of work, he frequently was in trouble.

"'Come, come,' said he to Olè one day, 'I see that matrimony does not agree with you very well. Let us have a bit of fun together.'

"So they started off together, and flew from tree to tree, chattering, pecking a wild berry or so, until night drew on, and they were far from home. They decided to sleep in a tamarind-tree, and pursue their way like good travellers before

the sun rose. They gathered themselves up into
soft little balls, with their heads sunk in a ruff
of feathers, and were soon fast asleep. About
midnight Olè awoke with a sudden start. He
could hear the owls hoot, and see the great bats
dart about after their evening meal of moths,
while the howling monkeys gave their peculiar,
ringing cry even now and then. Was this all?
No, there was a slight rustling, and he beheld in
the darkness two round globes of green fire slowly
approaching him. Olè knew that it must be a
hungry leopard, or some other member of the cat
tribe, yet he could do nothing but gaze at these
glowing balls, fascinated by their cruel beauty.
The black, crouching form came nearer and
nearer, each velvet paw treading the branches so
softly as to make no sound, until he felt the hot
breath hissing between the sharp teeth. He
uttered a quick cry of alarm, which served to
arouse his sleepy brother-in-law, and the two took
flight to a higher perch, just as the leopard prepared to pounce upon them.

"'That is not so bad,' said the brother-in-law,
in a drowsy tone, after they had settled them-

selves. 'I could tell you of a much worse time I had once. But come, let's have another nap.'

"'Not I!' said Olè. 'Do you suppose I will be caten if I can help it?'

"'Well, then,' returned the other coolly, 'you just keep watch, and let me know if you hear any thing.' So saying, he was soon snoring again, but Olè never closed an eye before the bell-bird began to toll out its wild, sweet note, in the early morning mists.

"The two parrots went on, getting into trouble enough, but always managing to just escape harm. One day they heard a great noise in the distance, and Olè thought he had never heard such a chattering, shrieking, and bellowing, in all his life.

"'An army of apes is coming to attack some plantation,' said the brother, looking very grave.

"Onward they came, and soon Olè could see them leaping from tree to tree, the leader directing their march, and the young ones scampering after. The two parrots hid themselves in a shrub, hoping to escape notice in the thick foliage, but a mischievous little ape caught a glimpse of Olè's top-knot, and pounced upon him. The brother-in-law flapped his wings and flew away; but Olè was so terrified that he could only drop to the ground, and creep into a hole near by. Poor Olè was in a sad state of terror, for he dared not fight the ape, and he also heard a strange hissing noise like that of several serpents in the den where he had taken refuge.

" 'If I was any thing but a parrot, I could get away. Fairy Linia, Fairy Linia,' he cried, taking a bead in his beak, and tossing it toward the sun, 'I wish I was a Hoonuman monkey.'

" Instantly he felt his feathers shrink, his body increase in size, and become covered with soft, gray fur, while his four little paws and face were black as velvet. Thus changed, he lost no time in scampering up out of the snake-hole, when he met the inquisitive ape face to face.

" 'How did you come all the way from India?' said he, rubbing his nose, and staring at Olè.

" 'Never you mind; I shall be back there soon enough,' returned the latter.

" 'Would you enjoy robbing a plantation with us, as long as you are here?' said the ape, then, as Olè declined, he ran off to join his company.

OLÈ AS THE SACRED MONKEY.

" The brother parrot fluttered near, in search of his lost comrade; but when he saw a monkey with a roguish black face instead, he spread his wings and flew home. This was the last Olè saw of him, or, indeed, any others of the family; for he never even went to bid his striped wife good-by, so she may be living a widow to this day. He next felt for the crystal box, which was concealed in the soft fur of his throat, then he fell into a deep sleep.

" When he awoke, he found himself in a great banyan-tree, whose branches had taken root and again sprouted, until the network of fibres spread in all directions. Olè rubbed his eyes, and looked about him curiously. The tree was on the outskirts of an Indian town, where he could see Hindoos bearing water-jars upon their bronzed shoulders, soldiers in scarlet uniforms, and elephants parading the streets with their riders in houdahs. About Olè were numerous others of his race, some scolding, some eating, the old ones strutting around, and the young ones cutting capers.

" Now the Hoonuman or Entellus monkey is

held sacred in India, for the Hindoos believe that the souls of their friends enter these animals after death, so that they are never allowed to be killed or injured.

"Oh, what a glorious life it was to be a monkey! that of a parrot was nothing to it. All Olè need do, was to make merry the whole time; he could walk the streets, perch on doorsteps, in fact do whatever he pleased, well knowing that the patient Hindoos would not resent his impudence. There was one young monkey with whom he became intimate, and this new companion proved to be the drollest fellow imaginable. Olè and he constantly went about in search of fun. They climbed upon casements, they rifled the pockets of Europeans, they tormented the shop-keepers, and chattered under the very noses of the highest dignitaries of the land, like the saucy creatures they were. Olè soon became the wildest of all Hoonumans, and the older ones had to remonstrate with him. It did no good, however, for he still would play his pranks on every one.

"One day the two friends were strolling along, when they concluded to enter the open door of a fine mansion. In they went to find a large, cool hall, with an English gentleman asleep in a hammock, and a native servant seated upon a mat. The two monkeys made themselves at home; one went to a table, ate a biscuit, and sipped some wine from a goblet, which he let fall while trying to drink like a gentleman, and the other attempted to use a chiboque, but, not knowing how, he wound the long stem about his neck for a collar instead of smoking it. The poor servant, fearing to awaken the sahib, tried to catch the intruders, when, to his astonishment, Olè leaped up into the hammock, tweaked the sleeper's nose, and pulled his whiskers. The English gentleman awoke with an alarming growl, and, beholding a pert young monkey seated upon his chest, he seized him by the nape of the neck, and began to whip him with a cane. Olè howled lustily at this treatment, while his friend scampered off out of danger. The gentleman then whistled, and a great dog came bounding in.

"'Now, Dash,' said he, 'you watch this rascal that he does not run away, for I shall shoot him this evening in the garden.'

"The dog wagged his tail to show that he understood every word, and presently Olè was left alone with this terrible guardian. And a sorry time he had of it too. If he moved so much as a paw, the dog showed all his teeth, so the poor monkey had to sit crouched up into a little bundle, trembling with fear lest he should be pounced upon. He had half a mind to change himself into some animal large enough to crush the dog, but he liked his present mode of life so much, he thought he would wait to see what came of it all.

"Now the Hindoo servant felt it was wicked to kill the monkey, and so deep is this feeling among his nation, that many a time the crack of a sportsman's gun at one of these sacred animals has produced open rebellion. Accordingly the servant came into the room where poor Olè crouched, and made a pretence of feeding the dog, that the monkey might escape. Olè lost no time in clambering out the window, up to a high wall; but he did not reach this place of safety before the dog had jumped after him, and bitten off the end of his tail. 'Worse things might have happened,' said Olè to himself, while he sat at his ease on the wall and examined the injured organ, 'for I have heard of some of my race that gnawed their own tails for the want of better amusement.'

"He finally reached the banyan-tree in safety, after having hopped upon a lady's shoulder and frightened her into a swoon, slapped a baby in the face, and pushed over a whole fruit-stand.

"Time went on, and Olè found that even a Hoonuman monkey must pay for his pranks sometimes. He was awakened one night by something cold touching him. All the neighboring monkeys set up a shrill chatter of alarm; he tried to move, but was held fast in the coils of a snake! Olè clutched at his crystal box, tossed out a bead, and cried: —

"'Fairy Linia, Fairy Linia, only change me to a Jungla tiger.'

"True to the Fairy's power, he was at once transformed to a beast, second only in its terrible strength of the animal kingdom. The branch upon which he had rested could no longer bear his weight, — it broke; Olè sank to the ground, and, shaking off the snake, which was in reality small, he sprang away through the darkness to the jungle. Now he had found the life he liked best, for he already felt the fiercer instincts of a wild animal. He made his way through the night-shadows to join his fellows. When morning dawned he was eager to see himself, so he went to the river, leaned over, and looked in.

" He was a magnificent creature, about four feet high, with golden-hued fur striped with a darker shade, white ears, and brilliant, yellow eyes, always changing and contracting. Olè contemplated his deep chest, powerful claws, and wide mouth with satisfaction.

" ' I am now one of the mighty animals of the earth, for I can equal the lion and the wild bull in strength. Who would not rather be a tiger than either a parrot or a monkey?' he said.

" How this newly changed tiger revelled in his power! He learned to track his food, and wait a chance patiently for hours to spring upon it, whether it was an antelope, a horse, or a man; then, after gorging himself with their flesh, seek some safe refuge to sleep away the ill effects of the feast.

" You may wonder how the boy could have been so altered, yet thus it was, the Fairy Linia made him for the time a brute and nothing else.

" He did not confine his ravages to the forest alone, but would enter towns boldly, causing the poor natives to flee before him, for none had the courage to slay him. At such times he frequently carried away a live ox with as much ease as if it had been a kitten, and sometimes women or children. Once he attempted to enter a hut where an old woman lived; but, finding the door barred, he leaped upon the roof, tore up the covering, and descended into the room that way. He found the old woman had, by that time, barred the door outside instead of in, and had run away, so he gained nothing.

" In India the foreign residents delight in the dangerous sport of tiger-hunting, and Olè had to take his share. He had stretched himself for repose in a safe cover of reeds, one day, when he was aroused by shouts and cries in the distance.

He raised his head to listen, and just then another tiger crept near for concealment.

"'It is a hunting party; we had better keep quiet here, and we may punish them yet,' said the new arrival, and the two mighty beasts laughed together over it.

"Presently there appeared a train of elephants, their riders armed to the teeth, followed by a band of natives, whose place it was to rouse the tigers by a clamor. Among the hunters was a lady, who held her fire-arms ready, her face expressive of eager excitement.

"'Ho, ho!' said Olè to his comrade. 'A woman come to hunt *us*. Have your eye on her; she seems a dainty morsel.'

"The criers beat the jungle, the elephants scented the breeze with trembling limbs for fear, the hunters fired a random shot or two, yet the two tigers never moved, but with glowing eyes and panting chests waited their time. The brave lady ordered her elephant wheeled nearer, leaned forward with a pistol ready, when the front of the houdah gave way, and she was thrown to the ground within three yards of where Olè crouched, lashing his sides with his tail. In another instant Olè was standing over the lady, binding her to the earth with his great paws. The shot rattled like hail about him, yet he never stirred, but, opening wide his huge jaws, prepared to devour her. Suddenly his teeth clenched together again, and some invisible power drew him back into the cover. The Fairy Linia would not suffer him to devour the lady huntress, so she led him away even against his will.

"Olè was not destined to range the forest always, for he was caught at last in a network of vines very cleverly, and led far away from his savage home. He was taken on board a ship, in an iron-bound cage, where he was fed by a man of whom he grew very much afraid. Do you know why? The man tamed Olè to submission by touching him with a red-hot rod of iron until he obeyed; so that, when he should be on exhibition, the tiger would always fear this torture.

"When they arrived at a foreign land, Olè was placed in a menagerie with lions, elephants, zebras, bears, and other animals. Soon the Jungla tiger attracted crowds of people to his cage, where he paced up and down, and glared at them through the bars. Finally he devised a cunning plan, as he thought. He gnawed a hole secretly in his cage, loosened some bars, and by covering the place with his large body managed to conceal it from his keepers. The next day, when the menagerie was crowded, a sudden shriek of terror rang upon the air, for the great Jungla tiger had escaped from his cage, and stood in the midst.

"What a commotion there was! The people trampled each other in their haste to escape, the other beasts roared, the keepers rushed about to secure the animal. Olè sprang into the crowd, tossed up a bead from the magic box, and muttered,—

"'Fairy Linia, Fairy Linia, I beg to be made a soldier-crab.'

"Rendered invisible for a time, Olè next found himself a wary, impudent little fellow enough, in one of the many tide-pools which line the sea-shore. His condition was as different as it well could be from that of the great animal he had so recently been. He now had sharp claws,

OLÉ AS THE SOLDIER CRAB.

a head well protected in armor, and two funny little black eyes, which seemed to squint different ways at once. He carried his home upon his back, and could retire into it at any time.

" 'After all, a crab is very independent, since he does not have to ask a night's lodging of anybody,' said Olè.

" The quiet tide-pool was not much to his mind, the tops and periwinkles which lived there were stupid, he thought, so he decided to wander forth. He sidled out into the bed of the ocean, enjoying his new roving life not a little, yet always keeping a keen look-out, for he knew he would be beset by many dangers. He liked his castle very well, still he thought he might as well have his wits about him, in case he should see another that would suit him better. Sure enough he discovered a fine large shell, apparently empty, so he went up to it, and thrust in a feeler to explore, when out popped an angry little crab to defend his home.

" 'I did not know you were there,' said Olè.

" 'Did you not, indeed!' retorted the other, in sharp tones. 'Come, do you want to fight?'

"He then snapped his claws in Olè's face, by way of a challenge; so the two went at it; rolling over, tussling and boxing each other, until they were fairly out of breath.

"'There, that will do,' said the angry little crab, a good deal flustered by this time, and they parted.

"Olè next came across the *maia-squinado* crab, who is one of the best scavengers of the sea, for with his voracious appetite he devours all food that would taint the purity of the water, and thus injure other animals. Olè regarded him with curiosity, for he had heard of him before. The squinado was seated under a rock, twiddling his feelers for the want of better amusement, and a prickly, dirty fellow he was, with spindle shanks and a round body.

"'How are you, Squinado?' said Olè.

"'Oh! my digestion is good as ever, thank you. I am feeling rather sleepy now, for last night I was at work upon a stale haddock until daybreak.'

"'Could you tell me where to find a new house? mine is rather rickety,' pursued Olè.

"'Let me think,' returned Squinado, who was very good-natured, although not at all handsome. 'It occurs to me that behind yonder rock you will see a whelk-shell, which might answer.'

"Olè thanked him, and went on as directed until he discovered the whelk-shell, which proved to be untenanted. Do you suppose that the soldier-crab inserted his body into this new covering at once? Not at all. He was altogether more prudent than that, for, while doing so, he could have easily been surprised by another soldier, who would readily have killed him. He first probed the shell carefully, then holding the old home firmly with one claw, he entered the other, tried it a little, then concluded he did not fancy it much, and returned to his first house again. His attention was attracted by a colony of anemones clustered upon a dark rock, which contrasted finely with their delicate coloring. These sea-flowers, harmless as they appeared, with their tentacles waving idly on the current, he knew to be dangerous foes, for, when any passing atom or animal touched these nerve-like threads, the whole fringe was quickly wreathed about, and the victim engulfed in the capacious stomach.

"'Good-morning, my pretty friends,' said Olè mockingly. 'I hope that none of you are very hungry.

"'Not at all, my dear crab,' returned a cream-colored zoöphyte, marked with blue rings and pink stripes. 'We have all had our breakfast.' With this the anemone stung Olè with one ten-tacle, but he skipped back nimbly. 'Not so fast,' he laughed, dancing just beyond their reach. 'I am not quite ready to be packed into your carpet-bags yet.'

"Olè began to enjoy this life immensely, for the spice of danger added a charm. He had become so skilful a warrior by this time that you will not wonder at what I am about to relate. A fine shell came in his way, with an anemone growing upon the top, and the inmate feeding quietly upon some meat. Quick as thought Olè pounced upon his unfortunate relative, dragged him out, put himself into the other's house, and trotted off, without at all minding the cruelty of the proceeding. Now, although he was so fierce with other crabs, in some cases he was better-natured.

" He might easily have torn the anemone from the roof of his shell, or injured the cloak anemone, that lined the entrance of his dwelling with its folds; but, instead, he carried them both along, and was the best of friends with them as well.

"He also allowed a beautiful marine worm to live in one of the recesses of his habitation, and this companion must have been a trial to his patience surely; for, whenever the crab fed, the worm came gliding out, and seized the morsel just as the 'soldier' prepared to swallow it. Strange to say, Olè seldom resisted; but sometimes he would start suddenly, and thus frightened the worm for a time, so that it would hide. The zoöphyte on Olè's back was a tough traveller, and so used had it become to many tumbles and jostlings in its journeyings with the crab, it never noticed bumps which would have crushed its more delicate brothers of the rocks. This anemone, upon learning that Olè had never been in that region before, promised to show him any thing interesting they should meet. Presently Olè's attention was attracted to the lima's nest.

" It was a coral grotto, rough outside the better to elude the glance of prowling enemies, but cemented together firmly and arranged within, by the wonderful skill of the inmate, so as to be a snug dwelling. The lima is a house-mason, and a rope-spinner besides. The walls are rendered smooth as plaster by a woven yarn, mingled with slime, the rough fragments of coral are bound together to resist the action of the waves, and smoothed in order not to injure the delicate mollusk, with its beautiful, white, ribbed shell, and yellow and pink fringed mantle.

" ' I envy you, Lima,' said Olè, peeping into the grotto.

" ' Yes, it is pleasant to live here,' said the lima, in a sweet little voice, ' but then one is always in fear of one's life, when out taking the air.'

" Some time after the striped anemone said, —

" ' We had better be careful now, for we are near a velvet fiddler, I believe.'

" The anemone had scarcely put Olè upon his guard, when out rushed the fiddler from a dark nook, like the Giant Grim from his castle. His red eyes, claws marked with blue and scarlet, and velvet, brown back showed him to be a very handsome crab, though a fierce one, as the dead bones strewn about the mouth of his cave exhibited. Olè managed to save himself by shrinking into his shell, where the fiddler could not reach him, and, as the former was diverted to a small fish just then, Olè was glad to scuttle off and escape.

"'I envy the velvet fiddler, too, for he is more powerful than I,' he thought to himself.

"But, if he had admired the lima and the fiddler, how much greater was his delight when he saw a wonderful creature swimming towards him! Its body was transparent, with darker markings, its eyes sparkling and brilliant, its legs slender and ornamented by yellow and blue bands, and its tail shaped like a fan. It darted through the water gracefully, and looked down saucily upon Olè, as if conscious of his admiration.

"'Well, what do you think of me?' said the prawn, for such it was.

" 'You are very handsome,' returned Olè politely.

" 'Why, I believe I am rather more elegant than my cousin the lobster, or my brother the shrimp. But do not judge of my beauty until I clean myself, I am really shockingly dirty.'

" So saying, the prawn led the way to a convenient place, and began to scrub himself with a pair of slender legs, and little pincer-like hands, with which he was furnished. He picked every particle of sand from his coat with these nail-brushes, and seemed to enjoy the process very much, for a prawn loves to be clean.

" 'I envy you,' said Olè, watching him with interest.

" 'You had better not,' replied the prawn, scouring one leg, 'I have hosts of foes. Among these, men delight to catch me, and, if they do not boil and eat me, they put me into a large glass box, that they may watch my habits, and flare candles in my face, when I ought to·be asleep, just to see how I take it all.'

" Olè went on his way, pondering over what he had seen, until he came to a cave. He looked into the twilight darkness of the place a moment, then turned to go, when he was suddenly arrested by a long, undulating band darting out of a crevice, and coiling about him.   The crab struggled: another arm shot forth to aid the first one.

"'It is a cuttle-fish,' whispered the cloak anemone.

"Soon Olè could see the terrible creature, which is merely a mass of jelly, with two large, indistinct eyes, the body surrounded by eight tentacles, like the spokes of a wheel. This Medusa, without bones or armor, has as great power to kill as any animal of the earth or sea, for its long arms wind tightly about its prey, and the many mouths suck the life-blood.

" Olè, terrified by the hidden dangers lurking beneath the waters, felt his shell crush in the slimy folds of the monster's embrace. He slipped a bead from the box, and called upon the Fairy Linia, in a drowning voice, for aid, with strength almost spent by the suffocating power of the cuttle-fish.

"'I wish I were a white dromedary.'

" In another moment the cuttle-fish loosened his

grasp, and sank to the bottom, with head severed from body, and Olè became insensible to every thing save a confused, rushing noise in his ears.

" When he recovered himself, he was standing in the vast, open desert, with nothing visible as far as the eye could reach, but waves of burning sand, and the clear sky above. When he attempted to move, he felt very strangely indeed. He had four long legs, cloven nostrils, slender neck, and a large hump upon his back, which would be a kind of stored provision to feed his system when no other food offered, and which also would enable the rider to sit at ease. He wandered about, cropping a few thistles and briers, which seemed to him delicious morsels, but he found it very lonely to be where there was no sign of life. Finally he saw the most beautiful lake of water in the distance, which reflected drooping trees and passing shadows, until he fancied he could see the ripples on the surface, and hear their plash against the pebbles of the shore.

" ' I never heard that one could find such cool, fresh lakes in the desert,' thought Olè, and

OLE AS THE DROMEDARY

started toward it; but the nearer he seemed to approach the farther away it grew, until his very limbs ached with weariness, and he was obliged to pause. What was this delusive sheet of water? It was the mirage of the desert, produced by the heated layers of air reflecting upon the yellow sand so as to form this cruel deception to the weary traveller.

" When Olè paused, he heard a distant tinkling sound, from the west, and presently he saw a dark line traversing the space towards him. The caravan happened to halt near by, so that he could see the trains of camels, horses, and mules, the gayly colored tents pitched for the wealthy merchants, and the guards polishing their weapons to prepare for the attack of midnight robbers. Olè wondered at the many different races he could distinguish among the travellers: here an old Jew, with ragged turban, fed his mule; here a swarthy Afghan, in robes of cashmere and silk, smoked a silver-mounted pipe; and there a Moslem bowed toward the East in his evening devotions.

"While Olè drew near shyly, to observe all these

things, several people saw him, and quickly started in pursuit of so handsome an animal as a stray white dromedary. All mounted their fastest camels or horses to give chase, except one young man, who had only a poor, little donkey to ride at all. This young man, whose name was Achmet, had been travelling to Babylon, in hopes of earning something for his parents who were very poor indeed. He now came forward, looking wistfully at Olè, and thinking how splendid it would be to own a dromedary, yet feeling it to be useless attempting to catch the animal when all the others were mounted.

" ' We will agree that the one who first throws a halter over the dromedary's neck shall own him,' said a Turk, who rode an Arabian horse; so away they started, leaving poor Achmet, of course, far behind. Now the dromedary is the fleetest animal in the world, because it can bear the greatest amount of fatigue, and Olè led them a pretty race over the desert, until even the Arabian horse was flecked with foam. He contrived to wheel about just when they were near, and, outstretching them all by his long, easy strides, he approached the astonished Achmet, and fell upon his knees before him. By the time the riders came up, Olè stood meekly with Achmet's halter over his neck, prepared to serve his new master. The rest grumbled, but could do nothing.

"The young man was so delighted with his prize that, after feeding and petting Olè for a time, he went to sleep with the dromedary's soft wool serving him for a pillow. The caravan toiled through the tedious journey, Olè bearing his new master with ease.

"Finally they approached their destination, the great city of Damascus. They wound along the highway, bordered by gardens of delicious fruits and flowers, then entered the city gate, and soon were in the thronged streets. Olè thought he had never seen any thing so magnificent as the open bazaars of silks, spices, and sweetmeats, the caparisoned mules, figures of male and female slaves bearing caskets of jewels and rich stuffs, and the marble palace of the sultan, surmounted by four domes, rising like golden bubbles over the city spires and roofs.

Achmet's father was a poor water-carrier, who was obliged to toil all day, carrying earthen jars from a well of fresh water. Achmet, by loading Olè, soon made enough to buy a mule, which aided his father very much. Olè delighted in the new life. He made many journeys to foreign cities, and, by his swiftness, many a time saved Achmet from robbers, for he had begun to trade in merchandise.

"At length the sultan Al-Abbas received the King of Persia as his guest, and for his entertainment ordered a great race at his country palace, when he would give a prize to the swiftest animal, whether horse or camel. All the city was in a state of excitement, as the time drew nigh. The great day arrived, the sun shone clear and bright, the multitude thronged out the city gates to watch the race from a distance, while the royal guard were drawn up before the palace walls, their armor glittering, and their gorgeous mantles fluttering in the breeze. Under a pavilion of cloth of gold, upon a divan of velvet, sat the sultan Al-Abbas and the King of Persia, both of them wearing turbans studded with jewels. In a silver casket before the sultan was placed the prize, which consisted of a gold box set with emeralds and pearls, and containing a diamond as large as a hazel-nut. Behind the lattice of the windows, the sultana and her court surveyed the scene.

"The gates were thrown open, each rider dismounted to salute the sultan, then they drew up in line, waiting for the signal to start. Among them was Olè, his coat freshly washed until it was white as snow, a string of silver bells about his neck, and a saddle of leather stamped with gilt figures.

"The sultan waved his right hand, the horses started, their hoofs flashed in the air, the camels followed, and soon all were out of sight. Olè found he had a powerful rival in a brown dromedary, ridden by a Jew, that kept pace with him long after the horses were outstripped. Achmet, all excitement, urged his animal onward, and Olè strained every nerve forward. They turned the curve of the race-course,— and the white dromedary began to flag.

"'O Fairy Linia, help me!' panted Olè.

"He felt a thrill through his frame, a new strength in every limb, and with long strides he reached his rival's side, from which he had previously fallen back. They could see the palace again, distinguish the mass of people, and the gilded diadem above the sultan's pavilion. They were very near, when Olè, gathering all his strength, sped forward and knelt before the throne, amid the applause of the multitude. Then Achmet received the silver casket with its precious contents, while all the others frowned with envy over his good fortune.

"Achmet soon after sold the great diamond to a prince of Syria for a great sum, which enabled him to build a palace as grand as that of the sultan himself. Olè was treated with great honors, having won all this wealth. His manger was made of marble, and his trappings of gold and velvet.

"All these glories he was enjoying, when one night a robber came to his stall, and led him out silently. Olè tried to escape, tried to make some sound, but could not, for the robber muzzled his nose quickly. The man then took the gold which he had stolen from Achmet's palace, mounted the dromedary, and rode away out of the city swiftly.

" Now it happened that a slave, hearing some noise, had peeped out of a window into the court-yard, and seen the robber upon Olè's back, so he alarmed the household. Soon the robber found he was pursued, and urged the dromedary for-ward with all speed. Olè bethought him of a way to punish him, by slackening his pace until the pursuers were near; then he said, —

" ' Fairy Linia, Fairy Linia, I should like to be a white eagle.'

" The dromedary vanished suddenly, leaving the robber an easy captive, for he could not then escape.

" Olè next found himself upon the rocky sum-mit of a high mountain, where he could see the world of valleys and rivers spread far below him. With his keen gaze he watched the feathered tribe beneath him, the snowy sea-gulls sailing slowly toward their homes, the ducks paddling about, the silent cranes standing watchfully by some pool, and the shrieking, chattering crows.

In his superior strength and greatness, Olè
laughed at them all. He snapped his strong
beak, and ruffled his handsome feathers, proud
of his own glory.

"Just then his attention was drawn to a hawk
that hovered over the sea for a moment, then,
darting swift as an arrow downward, vanished in
a whirl of foam, to re-appear bearing a fish in its
mouth. Olè swept from his perch to attack the
hawk, and soon there ensued a battle in mid-air.
The two powerful birds wheeled about, clashing
their heavy wings, and startling the echoes with
their sharp clamor. Finally the hawk let go his
hold, the fish dropped, when Olè pounced upon it
and bore it to his eyry to devour at leisure.

"The eagle did not confine himself to robbing
hawks, but captured smaller birds, hares, and
even deer, with his cruel beak and claws.

"How long Olè might have led this life, I do
not know, had he not one day espied a lamb,
which had strayed from the flock into the woods.
Olè wheeled above the poor, little animal, but
the thick branches of the trees prevented his
making a direct descent. The lamb started

upon seeing him, and, fearing to lose the prey, the bird made a swoop among the boughs, hoping to break them with his weight; but instead he caught the gold cord which held the crystal box about his neck; it broke, scattering the remaining four beads to the ground.

" Olè felt himself seized, bound, and whirled through the air, a heavy darkness settling over him.

" After that, he was shut in the crystal box for a punishment by the Fairy, a very long time. Although it was tedious enough lying there, Olè had time to think of many things, and make some very good resolutions for the future. Finally the Fairy let him out, and summoned him before her throne.

" ' You have now been a parrot, a monkey, a tiger, a crab, a dromedary, and an eagle,' said she. 'If you prefer being changed to any of these, I will do it.'

" ' If you please,' replied Olè in an humble tone, ' I would rather be what God made me, after all.'

" So the Fairy Linia released him, and he rose

to the surface of the sea once more, where, to his surprise, he found his little boat rocking on the waves, with the bag of feathers in it. He rowed home to find that he had only been gone a day. How many adventures he had had in that short space of time!"

"He presented his feathers to Dame Katrine, who made of them an excellent pillow. No one knew of his visit to the Fairy's court below the waves, but every one soon found that he deserved the title of 'discontented' no longer. He became cheerful and happy, and, when he grew to manhood, was so good a son to Claës that he loved him as much as any of his own children."

When the Teapot had finished, it fainted away, in the most graceful and ladylike manner. The Saucepan supported the insensible form, the Cricket applied a hot ember to the Teapot's nose as a smelling bottle, and the Kettle tried to leap down from the hook, boiling with sympathy. Finally the Teapot revived a little, for the Cricket had made a fan out of a scrap of paper, which was of infinite service.

"I think the heat overcame me," said the Teapot in a faint voice.

"Your story was splendid," said the Kettle, who had in reality dozed through half of it, and had but a faint idea of what Olè had been about the whole time.

"Which of all his changes did you like best?" said the Cricket sharply, for he more than suspected that the president had been asleep.

"Why, they were all so good, I hardly know," replied the Kettle, rubbing one eye in a puzzled manner.

The next evening the Teapot felt better, although she still complained of a slight headache. They were all curious to know what the Saucepan would do, in her turn, particularly as she had burned every thing she attempted to cook the day before. She arranged herself with an important air, and commenced:—

6

THE OAK-TREE'S STORY.

———◆———

"I WAS born in a beautiful forest glade of the Apennines, where you may see many of my brothers waving their giant branches above all smaller trees, graceful ferns, and grasses, and the little sparkling brook that sings through the valley all day long.

"Here I was born from a tiny acorn, as I have said; but do you know that all this rustling forest was once only a barren rock surface, and that the lichens first grew their rough mantle over the hard stone, then were succeeded by a soft bed of mosses, that by their decay spread a layer of earth, in which seeds scattered by passing birds took root, to spring and flourish to the growth you now behold?

"Here I always have lived, for I have no

power to go hither and thither when I wish, as you can: my roots are fixed too firmly in the earth for that. No, I must stay in this one spot, and get what pleasure I can from what surrounds me, and that is not a little, I assure you. When the sun rises and touches my leaves with his first golden rays, I awake from a refreshing sleep, and begin to wonder what will happen this day.

"First the birds that build their nests in my branches, who have been chippering away briskly since daybreak, come back with the breakfast they have hunted for their hungry young ones, and tell me the news.

"'The beech-tree sends you a good-morning,' pipes a robin politely.

"Or a woodpecker comes trotting up my trunk like a mouse with a grave, dignified air, and taps me with his long, sharp bill. I have a great respect for the woodpecker, you must know, for he is the doctor among trees. He goes to work just as a physician might by feeling your pulse, and looking at your tongue. He gives us a rap or two, and, if we are sound, trots off again;

but, if we are diseased, he bores away a hole, and eats the grub which will soon destroy us. This is what the little woodpecker has been made for by a good God, although the ignorant suppose he drills all trees alike, and thus injures them. I must confess I am a trifle afraid of him; when he makes me a visit, I always fancy he may find me out of health; however, I generally ask what he has seen in his travels.

"'Oh!' he will say, giving me a sharp peck the while, 'your neighbor to the left is in a very bad way, I have fed my whole family out of him this long time.'

"Later in the day the swineherd comes along with his flock of grunting pigs, who stand under my boughs, winking their little red eyes and wagging their curly tails, as if begging me to throw them a sweet acorn or two; so I just shake myself, and down pelts the shower into their hungry mouths.

"Or perhaps some tired traveller rests in my shade from the hot sun, and I wave my leaves gently that their soft music may lull him to sleep.

"Many years ago a wayworn pilgrim paused beside me, and, leaning on his staff, gazed about him. He was a very old man, with a long, silver beard, and wearing the woollen robe and knotted cord of a monk. He never left me afterward. He made himself a home in the arched hollow of my trunk, which was large enough to form a shrine for a crucifix. He made a bed of dried leaves, on which he slept. Soon his fame spread through all the country round, as a hermit of great sanctity, and the people brought gifts to place before him, fruits, flowers, and food; but he left all these to the birds, for the hermit lived upon bitter herbs and roots, which he gathered day by day, and drank of the clear water of the brook.

"There lived, upon a hillside near, a vine-dresser, who was a good man, and who had a little daughter named Lizette. The cottage where they lived was built upon a ledge of rock, high above the valley, and approached by a narrow, winding path. Lizette was all the little house-keeper her father had, for her mother had died of the fever when she was a very young child, and she early learned to prepare their frugal meals, then watch for his return from the vine-yards, when the sun was setting in the west. One day she heard, from a neighbor's child, of the hermit that lived in the oak-tree, and she wished to see the holy man; so she prepared a wheaten loaf and a flask of wine, then entreated her father to go to the forest with her. Perhaps you may wonder how I should know so much of the vinedresser's daughter, rooted as I am in the valley; but I might readily do that, for the flowers whispered when she was coming, the birds twittered her name, and the very sunbeams lingered lovingly about her path, shedding stray drops of gold upon her fair head.

" The hermit was roused from his meditations by the little girl, who modestly offered her loaf and wine. A smile lighted up his face; he blessed her, and gave her a sacred relic from another land, which he bade her suspend about her neck. After that Lizette came to visit the hermit often, sometimes with her father, some-times alone; but she always had some little gift, such as a cluster of grapes or other fruits, of which he would partake since they came from her. Then he would tell her the wonderful legends of his Church, about the early saints and martyrs that perished at the hands of cruel men for Christ the Lord.

"But the summer sun will not shine always, you know, and, sure enough, the autumn winds began to play their pranks among my branches, and never ceased until they had stripped off all my leaves. Winter came with his train of storms and gales, yet the hermit still lived in the hollow of my tree, for he believed that by so doing he served God the better. Lizette visited him faithfully, to help him as she could. Sometimes in the night, when the stars were shining brightly, she would awaken in her warm little bed, and think of the hermit on his couch of leaves, exposed to the cold winds, with a heavy heart. Toward the spring-time a storm began, and I knew very well it would be a fearful one, for I had never seen the like before, and I was then pretty old. How the clouds lowered in black masses above us! How the rain poured in sheets for days together!

"I sheltered the hermit in my trunk the best I could, but even then he was drenched and shivering. At last the brook, which in summer only rippled along pleasantly, became larger and larger, foaming up over its banks, gathering strength with every drop of rain that fell, until it spread over the whole valley in a flood. The wind began to roar like a giant, tearing up shrubs, scattering branches, twisting and bending the stoutest trees, and all the while the waters rose. The hermit was obliged to leave his home near the ground, and climb to one of my branches. Inch by inch, slowly but surely, the stream rose, until the very tree-tops were covered. I could feel how it crept up my trunk, soon reaching the hermit, then following him higher and higher to the very top bough of my lofty height.

"For three days and three nights the flood raged, cottages floated past me on its surface, huge trunks of trees came floating down, while many animals struggled along, lowing piteously. For this long time he remained on my top branch, only just beyond the reach of the waters, that

occasionally washed over his feet, but came no
further. He had only a crust of Lizette's bread,
which he had taken when he mounted my trunk.
When the moon rose, the vinedresser and his
daughter looked down into the valley, where
nothing could be seen but ruin, and prayed for
the poor hermit, whom, they thought, must certainly be dead. No one could reach him, so
Lizette had to content herself with watching for
the waters to subside.

"At last the rain ceased, the sun peeped out
from a mantle of heavy clouds, and I felt the
flood creep down, leaving my trunk exposed
once more. Oh, how delightful was the warm
sunlight and air, after being surrounded by tur-
bid waters! I felt all my life and strength re-
newed again, as I stretched wide my strong
arms; but to the hermit, faint and weak from
hunger and cold, the sun brought no warmth.
He tried to reach the ground, but slipped and
fell. Just then the vinedresser and Lizette
came. They raised the poor old man, and put
wine to his lips, so that he opened his eyes once
more. He placed his hand upon the head of

6*

little Lizette, then, having blessed her, died. The vinedresser buried him under my shade, and his daughter wove garlands of wild flowers to place upon the grave.

"The years glided by over my head, and the woodpecker tapped me to see if I was sound in health, while little Lizette on the hillside was a child no longer, for she had grown to womanhood since the hermit died in the spring-time, and was now esteemed the fairest maiden in all the country round. Many were her suitors, but the vinedresser shook his head at them all. Pretty maids are not to be kept at home in that way.

"I heard the news at last, although it was some time in reaching me. A great, white owl had built its nest in the hermit's hollow after he died, and the bird became a friend of mine. Now although the expression is frequently used, 'wise as an owl,' still people seem to consider them but stupid things at the best. To be sure, if you disturb them in broad daylight, they stare blankly with great, dull eyes, and flap about clumsily, but at night it is quite a different thing; their eyes brighten, they dart swiftly after insects on the wing, and are all activity until day breaks, when they seek refuge in some dark nook again. Well, this one in my trunk was tiresome sometimes, for he delighted to hear himself talk, yet I liked him. I have told you before, I think, how the other birds gave me the news by daylight, but at night, when they are only sleepy, little balls of feathers in their nests, the owl found what the earth was about in the moonlight.

"One night he came flying home, in a state of great excitement, and wakened me out of a sound sleep, which made me rather cross.

"'Whoo! whoo!' said he, 'what do you think? Lizette, the vinedresser's daughter, is soon to be married.'

"'Who will she marry?' I inquired, my curiosity overcoming my ill-temper.

"'Oh, ho!' cried the owl, chuckling, and cocking his head sideways. 'Guess once.'

"'I am sure I do not know: the gardener at the castle, perhaps.'

"'No,' replied my friend, his eyes glowing like coals of fire in the darkness. 'Guess again.'

"'You must permit me to say first, sir,' I

remarked politely, ' that your eyes are very handsome in this light.'

" ' Thank you, my dear oak, for the compliment,' replied the owl, skipping on one leg. ' As you are so courteous, I must tell you without delay, it is the young cooper Lizette will marry. And now, as I have not much time before daybreak, you will excuse me if I search for a few more moths for supper.'

" So saying, he swept away into the night.

" Lizette married the young cooper, and a happy life they led near the vinedresser, whose heart was delighted by a little grandchild soon.

" The world was smooth and pleasant for all, when one day a party of woodcutters came to the forest. I hoped they would not notice me, but my turn had come at last. They girdled me about, and soon their sharp axes cut deep into my sides, while with every fresh wound the echoes sped away to my lofty brothers, telling them this would be their fate, sooner or later. I felt my hold in the ground growing weaker and weaker, I raised my proud head for the last time above the striplings about me, I wavered once, twice, then fell with a loud crash to rise no more.

"My remains were chopped up into lengths, and scattered about for the various purposes of man, and the young cooper fashioned from a part of me a large cask for wine. This cask stood near the house, and one day Lizette was seated near the door, with her youngest child upon her lap, and the other clinging to her dress. The soft wind caressed the beautiful group, the sunlight flickered over them, and the trees showered their pearly blossoms about them.

"A stranger passed by in the pathway, and paused to look at them. He was a young man, with a strange, dreamy look in his eyes, and long hair thrown back from his face. That face one and all of us can look upon, in almost every picture-gallery of the land: it was Raphael. His eyes lost their abstraction when they rested upon this mother and her children. He felt hastily about his person for paper, but could find none, then he took a piece of chalk, and sketched upon the cask-head the three portraits.

"Well," sighed the oak-tree, "all that remains

of my former glory is a log or so, thrown carelessly down in some workshop, and a few chips scattered on the winds, yet I shall always live in the minds of men, for from the drawing on the cask-head made of my wood was painted the great master's most beautiful picture of the Madonna."

The Saucepan was in great spirits over her tale, because she knew that none of them considered her very clever. They praised it highly, and the Kettle never snored once while she was telling it. The president's turn came next, and some delay ensued.

"It is no use," said the Kettle lazily, when they met. "I cannot tell another, for my brains are so thick I can remember nothing. If the Cricket would only tell the next now."

So the Cricket said he would, as he really liked to hear himself talk better than any thing else.

The story he gave was : —

OLD TOM'S FAMILY.

———◆———

"TOM and his wife were two excellent, middle-aged cats; she being of rather the higher family, for she had Maltese blood in her veins, while he was fat, sleek, and nothing more. Now Tom was very fond of his wife; but she also tried his temper sometimes, with her fine airs over her high connection.

"'Dear me,' she would say, licking her dainty white paws, 'what a show I could make in the city, where my uncle's family live! But then, where is the use of talking, when I have disgraced myself by marrying so much beneath me?'

"'Never despise a cat because of a rough coat,' the amiable Tom would reply; 'my heart is in the right place, I hope.'

"Tom's wife, beside the other advantages of

high birth, was of a very delicate and nervous temperament. She could not eat so much as a mouse-tail (which every cat knows is a delicious morsel) without a fit of indigestion; she could not even look at a dog without going into hysterics; and she had been known to faint away if her beefsteak was not properly cooked.

"It was fortunate for Tom that he lived in a comfortable country-house, for I do not know what would have become of his wife had they lived in fields and hedges, as so many cats do.

"But we must now describe the family. There they lay coiled up in a nice, warm basket, in the old attic, seven in number; all nestled together, so that you could not see much, but a black nose here, a white tail there, and a plump gray body or so. There never was a cat so delighted with his children as Tom. He frisked about their nest, trying to amuse them with odd bits of string; but they were too sleepy to notice him. After a time, though, they began to crawl out of the basket, and tried to use their weak little legs, which grew stronger daily, until they became as bright, pretty kittens as one would wish to see.

"Tom's wife began to complain of pains in her spine, and neuralgia in her right ear, and blindness in her left eye, and weakness of the lungs, until the cat-doctor, who had given her many wise medicines already, declared her to be sinking fast. Sure enough, Tom was finally left a melancholy widower.

"When the funeral was over he said to himself, 'I am still a young cat, yet I will never marry again, but will devote myself to my children.'

"He called them all to him, and seated himself in the circle, with his tail curled about his feet, and a very grave face. On his right was his eldest son, Dick, who was black as possible, with round green eyes; on his left his eldest daughter, Tabby, who certainly. was not at all handsome, having fur of a dingy yellow color, but then she was an excellent housekeeper. Next came Pet, a pretty, snow-white kitten, with a saucy little face and bright eyes; then Tiny, who was a beautiful Maltese, like her mother; then Tip, her twin-brother, a conceited young cat, very proud of his whiskers; then mischievous

Bob, already a capital mouser; then Tim, who was of no particular color, and always snarled at everybody. 'My dear children,' said Tom, sniffing violently to keep from crying outright, 'I shall never marry again.'

"'Pooh!' grumbled Tim, 'we shall have a step-mother in a month.'

"'Tim, be quiet,' said Tabby severely.

"Tim rumpled up his hair sulkily, and said no more.

"'It will be a long time before you will be able to leave home,' pursued the father, 'for you have no wisdom yet in the world's ways, so I shall hope to keep you under my eye until you are properly educated.'

"'My dear father,' remarked Dick coolly, 'I am thinking of making a journey very soon to see something new.'

"'I am sure, papa, you do not expect us to stay here always!' exclaimed Pet, cutting a caper.

"'Will you leave me so soon?' said Tom, with tears in his eyes. 'All I ask, then, is that you will return in a year from Christmas time to tell me your adventures.'

"So they promised, and one by one the kittens went out into the world to gain their own living.

"The year went by very slowly for Tom, who had begun to feel himself old and lonely. Finally the day came when his children should return, and they all appeared but one: little Pet was not among the number. Where could she be? Alas! no one knew. They left her place vacant in the circle, and put a bit of crape in her seat, supposing she must be dead. Then old Tom went away for a moment, and returned leading another cat by the paw.

"'This, my dears, is your new mother.'

"The kittens all looked at her in silence. She was plain and thin, with a long nose and yellow eyes.

"'I said we should have a step-mother,' snarled Tim.

"Even Tabby tossed her head, and said, 'I should not have married but for *this*.'

"'Bless me!' said Tiny, with a fashionable lisp, 'how could you marry such a fright, papa?'

The step-mother cat began to grow angry, her

tail wagged slowly, and her yellow eyes grew larger and larger, until they resembled globes of fire. The first thing she did was to box Tim on the ear very smartly, then she walked up to Tiny and slapped her in the face. What a hubbub arose! Miss Tiny seized the step-mother by the hair and knocked her cap off, Tim pulled her tail, Dick tweaked her nose for her, and she nearly scratched Tabby's eyes out the while. Poor Tom tried to silence the uproar as best he could. He miowed at his new wife, he howled at his children, but they were all far too busy pushing, scrambling, and scratching to notice him. At last the step-mother found she was getting the worst of it, so she jumped up to a window-seat, and began to cry.

" 'I wish I had never married again,' she sobbed. 'I was much better off as a widow.'

" At last Tom managed to quiet them by pointing out the piece of crape in Pet's place, which they had all trampled in their excitement. They then begged the step-mother's pardon, in rather a sulky way, and took their places again.

" ' Now, children,' said Tom, when order was

restored, 'I want to ask what each of you have done. Dick, you can begin.'

"'Excuse me,' replied Dick politely, 'I believe my sister Tabby should come first, as she is some three minutes older than myself.'

"'I do not know that I have much to tell,' began Tabby, folding her paws in a very proper way, 'still you shall have what there is to know. I stayed at home with papa for a time, intending to be a comfort to him when—' here Tabby paused and looked over her shoulder at the step-mother on the window-seat, who stared back quite fiercely in turn.

"'I thought I had better go away when papa married again,' she went on in a milder tone; so I travelled out into the world, I did not care much where. I went along the highway for some time until I saw a wagon lumbering toward me, and a great, ugly dog bounding along beside it. I felt my fur stand on end in an instant, for I must have some of my mother's dread of dogs, although I do not inherit her beauty, so I crept through the fence to hide. While I crouched under a rock listening and watching for what might come next, it began to rain heavily, and the thunder crashed through the trees above me until my teeth fairly chattered. Ugh! how cold and wet it was! I almost wished myself home again. The water trickled down my back, and my feet got so wet! If there is any thing I dislike, it is to be damp. Well, I will not weary you by telling what I suffered in that wretched wood, for I see that Bob. is laughing. At length I saw, to my surprise, a procession of cats coming slowly towards me, all with umbrellas over their heads, and water-proof cloaks upon their shoulders. When the leader came near, she looked at me with an impudent laugh, and I dare say I was a sorry figure crouched there under the rock.

" " " Where are you all going?" I said.

" ' The leader only tossed her head in a proud manner, but fortunately one of the others was kinder to me.

" " " The King of Catdom is choosing a wife for his eldest son, Prince Mowler," she said, " and we are all going to present ourselves at court to see if any of us will suit."

" " " I will have my chance, too," I said, and stepped along after them.

" ' At this they all giggled, but I kept my place without another word more until we reached our destination. We went through a cave, and then found ourselves at the gates of a splendid mansion. The entrance was guarded by two soldier-cats, wearing cocked hats and swords, who seemed half minded to thrust me out. We passed through a court yard and hall to a dressing-room, where there were a number of lady's maids in aprons and caps, who removed the cloaks of my companions, and stroked their coats into order. One of these maids came to me, and with her assistance I was soon as clean and dry as the rest, although they were all ever so much more beautiful.

" ' We were then conducted to the hall of audience, where the king was seated upon his throne, with his family about him. I noticed Prince Mowler at once, he had such fine eyes and long moustaches.

" " " You are all good-looking enough, except that yellow one," said the king, surveying us through his eye-glass, "but you must prove you have something else to recommend besides beauty before you marry Prince Mowler. To-morrow you shall each make me a soup, and the best one shall win the prize."

"'The cats all looked at each other in dismay; but I only laughed quietly to myself. That night I never slept a wink for thinking how I should make my soup, and early next morning I set about my work. The cooks gave each of us a kettle, and I took good care that none of my pretty companions should see what I was about. First I searched in the royal larder for materials, which I found very readily, as the king is fond of his dinner. What a dish I made of it! My mouth waters only to think of it. What was there in it? you ask. What was there *not* in it? There were bits of mutton, beef, and ham; a dozen whole mice, several radishes and onions sliced; a leaf of cabbage or so, half of a fish, a bit of cheese, some peppergrass, and ten rats' tails grated fine for a seasoning.

"'When the time came we each stood by our kettle, with white aprons on, and a ladle in our right paws, ready for the king. He tasted the soup of the leader, who had laughed at me only the day before, and made *such* a face! "Pooh!" he exclaimed, "it is nothing but dirty water." Then he tried the next one, and so on, until he came to mine, without any of them suiting at all. When he had dipped the ladle into my kettle, he was delighted beyond measure. He tested its flavor, snuffed the savory steam, and finally sat down before it and drank every drop, boiling hot as it was.

"'"You shall be my daughter-in-law," he said, wiping his whiskers when he had finished.

"'So I married Prince Mowler, of them all, and the pretty cats, who could not cook, went home again. My happiness did not last long, however,' concluded Tabby, with a sigh, 'for Prince Mowler was choked with a grasshopper's leg soon after our marriage. I am still a member of the royal household, and am esteemed the best cook in all Catdom. I must go home in time to preserve some young rats early in the season, before they get tough.'

"When Tabby had finished, her family could

7

do nothing but sniff in concert at the thought of her wonderful soup. As for the step-mother, she jumped down from the window, and shook hands (or paws rather) with the Princess Mowler. So they were good friends from that moment.

"Then old Tom requested Dick to give an account of himself.

"'I have not met the King of Catdom, or done any thing else extraordinary, sir,' said Dick, rubbing his chin in a thoughtful manner, 'yet I have had some queer times too. You all know that I am as sober as my sister Tabby, and I also have always desired to explore musty, odd nooks. I was born in this garret, which is certainly a very quaint place, with its rag-bags, old coats and hats, rusty bird-cages, and fishing-rods. When I started, I determined to visit any other such place I could.

"'I had not journeyed far when I saw a large, red brick building on a hillside, which I decided to enter. It was almost night when I slid through a chink by the gate, and had scarcely looked about me when two boys pounced upon me, and put me into a bag. I kicked and bit and snarled, but it did no manner of good, for they only laughed at me. I stayed in the bag so long a time that I fell asleep. I was roused by the boys again, and this time they took me out, and began to dress me up in a style which I hope none of you will ever try. They fitted walnut-shells upon my feet, tied a tin kettle to the end of my tail, and a string of fire-crackers to the kettle, then carried me to the top flight of stairs, and gave me a push down.

"'I shall never forget that moment.

"'My feet slid, my walnut-shell slippers clattered, the fire-crackers went fizz, bang! behind me, and the kettle rattled and bumped with such a din that all the teachers (for it was a school) came rushing out in their night-caps to see what in the world was the matter. The boys had gone to bed again, and pretended to be sleeping very hard indeed when the master came in his dressing-gown. The next morning no one could prove who had done the deed, for a cat cannot tell his own story, though I should have liked to, so the master just whipped them all round to make sure the right one did not escape.

"'I soon had a chance to help the master to discover more mischief. School-boys are always hungry, you know, and one night they made a nice plan to rob the housekeeper's storeroom, and have a feast. The boldest one went down stairs very softly when everybody was asleep, and came up again with a pie and some gingerbread. I had seen what he was about, so I just hid in the hall-window until he passed under me, then leaped down on his back with a loud hiss. How he jumped and screamed, letting fall the pie-dish with a crash! My goodness, what a time it made! The boys were not hungry again for a long time, I assure you. I have remained there ever since, for, as the housekeeper and master are very kind to me, I should not be apt to do better. I expect the boys would be glad to wring my neck if they could, but I take good care to keep out of their reach,.you had better believe. I have been troubled with corns ever since they fitted the walnut-shells, which were many sizes too small, upon my feet.'

"'If it is my turn next,' said Tiny, 'I shall leave it all to Tip, as we have been together all the time, and I am no story-teller besides.'

" 'Yes, Tiny and I have travelled together a long way,' said Tip, who had grown to be the very handsomest son of the family. 'We have seen many wonderful sights on the road, and at last we have suited ourselves exactly. We went in company because we are twins, and also Tiny is so pretty and delicate that I was afraid she would get hurt if left alone. You would not wonder at my fears for her, had you seen the battles I had to fight to prevent her being carried off, she is such a beauty. It seems only a wonder that my nose is not spoiled for life.

" 'We had walked many miles, and were feeling very tired, when we observed a high wall and a hedge, which looked so cool and pleasant in contrast to the hot, dusty road, that we entered the place. We found ourselves on the broad avenue leading to a beautiful house, surrounded by trees and flowers. A young lady was playing with a spaniel by a fountain, as we approached, and when she saw us she began to stroke Tiny, who immediately nestled into her arms without fear. We were taken into the house, and treated with every attention. We slept on velvet cushions, we played with balls on the soft carpets of the long parlors, and had nothing to do but grow fat and happy.

"'One day, while taking a walk, I met the gardener's cat, who was as gaunt and lean as I was sleek and plump. I took him home with me, and when we had eaten our dinner we gave him what was left. This we repeated every day until he grew as fat as we were. We then began to look about for other hungry neighbors, whom we fed with him. The young lady, our mistress, was much amused by our conduct, so she increased our allowance every day, and, as she increased, we added another hungry cat to the list of our dependents.

"'Tiny and I now feed twenty cats from our table. What do you think of that?' concluded Tip, with an important air.

"'I am delighted to have you generous, only don't think too much of your own goodness,' said Tom, with a warning shake of the head. 'Now, Bob, we will hear your story.'

"'Where is the use?' replied Bob slyly. 'I have done nothing wonderful, like my distinguished brothers and sisters. No, indeed: my year has been passed in ditches, on river-banks catching fish, or in search of field-mice, for I am a famous sportsman by this time. I roamed about the country after birds, and narrowly escaped being killed on several occasions; then I went to the city, where I took up my abode in an old mill, near the water's edge. I liked the miller very much, for he was always kind to me. To my sorrow, he sold the mill to a crabbed old man, and moved to another part of the city. The family took me with them to their new home; but, bless you! I could find no fun in it, every thing seemed so new and tame, so I scampered back to the mill again.

" 'My old master tried to coax me away, the cross new master kicked me about, yet I still liked my bed on a meal-bag, and my frolics among the mice at night. At last they gave up all hopes of ever seeing me, and, when they had done so, a curious event happened. The miller came in one Sunday morning with a lighted pipe, and after a time went away again. A spark must have fallen from the match, for soon after, while I was parading the lofts alone in my glory, a sudden shoot of flame crept up the wall, followed by clouds of dense smoke, and soon the mill was all ablaze. I had my tail singed for me before I managed to reach the ground in safety.

"'Now, thought I, what shall I do next? I have no friends here, and the dear, old mill is burned to the ground; the mice must be well roasted by this time, with no one to eat them,—the more's the pity! and the new miller does not care a straw whether I starve or not. Where had I better go? Why, to the church near by, of course, where my old master has been every sabbath for many a year, and wait for him there.

"' Accordingly I went to the church-door, and waited until he came out, then I rubbed myself against him, purred, and said, as plainly as a cat can, "Take me home." They none of them supposed I would stay, but I did very quietly and contentedly. When they heard that the mill was burned, they laughed at me for a clever puss, in seeking my best friends again. I shall go back to them when I leave here, but first I must have a scour round the country to get me into good health and spirits."

"'I shall get through what I have to say as quickly as possible, for I am dreadfully hungry, having had nothing to eat to-day, except a few beetles,' said Tim, who had only grown more surly and ill-tempered since he had left home. I also have been to town, like my brother Bob, although I saw nothing of him when I was there. I have lived in the wine-vaults, which wind away in long, dark passages under the houses. I like them, — they seem so black and grim; then, besides, if one has stolen a bit of meat from the butcher's shop around the corner, or taken another cat's dinner, one can hide there to eat at one's leisure. I don't like the porters that are always tramping in and out, rolling the casks about, and kicking poor me with their heavy boots. I have been so bruised and battered by barrels tumbled upon my back, being squeezed against the wall (that is the reason I am so thin), I never lose a chance of biting and scratching the porters. I believe I have said enough, that is if step-mamma will give me something to eat, for I am all but dead. I should invite you to visit me, father, but you are too old to dodge the casks, so you might have your head knocked off in no time.'

" The step-mother then set the table with all manner of good things, and when all the young cats found what a fine cook she was they liked her much better, for they all had excellent appetites. They had not been seated long at table, when they heard a quick patter of footsteps, and Pet sprang forward as snowy white as ever, with a pink ribbon about her neck, and a silver bell attached to it. What a time they made over her! They all embraced her at once, until she was nearly squeezed to death.

" ' There !' she exclaimed, ' you will spoil my ribbon entirely. Do let me have some pie, I am so tired.'

" So they helped Pet to pie, and took their places again.

" ' Who are you ?' said Pet suddenly, looking at the step-mother. ' Papa's housekeeper, I suppose.'

" ' Yes, my dear,' replied the step-mamma very mildly.

" Tabby then whispered to Pet, who stared, shook her head, then went on eating.

" ' How came you to get that bell ?' said Tiny; ' where I live, they are out of fashion.'

" ' Are they, indeed?' returned Pet, tinkling her bell; ' perhaps there are no cats pretty enough to wear them.'

" At this Tiny grew angry.

" ' We are pretty enough to sleep on silk cushions and roll on velvet carpets.'

" ' Do you have cream at eleven o'clock every morning?'

" ' Do you have twenty—' began Tiny, spitting at her sister across the table. Then old Tom interfered.

" At length the new arrival was ready to tell her adventures.

" ' A little servant found me in the street,' said Pet, ' and took me to the house where she lived. There were ever so many rosy little children in the nursery when she carried me in, and they all welcomed me cordially. I thought they never

would have been dressed for breakfast that morning; they did nothing but caper about me, as I
sat on the hearth-rug, this one with an odd boot
in his hand, that one dodging nurse just when
she attempted to tie a pinafore-string, until I
feared the poor woman would be crazed. Then
when the bell rang, and papa's voice sounded in
the hall, the children had to scamper away, leaving baby alone, who had already taken his meal
of bread and milk. Nurse put him on the hearth,
and we had a nice frolic together. First baby
tumbled, then I tumbled, and we rolled over each
other. I would frisk over baby where he lay
gurgling and laughing, sometimes walking right
upon his fat little face, but this I did very lightly,
taking care that my sharp claws did not hurt his
soft cheek.

"'We have led a merry life of it ever since, for
the children and I are the best of friends; we
never are very rough with each other, and if I
get tired of them I spring up on the mantel-piece,
or the bureau-top, to make grimaces at them for
a change. The reason I am late is because they
had a doll's tea-party, and I was dressed in a red

cloak, put into an armchair, and made to drink sweetened water out of a tiny cup. I did not like this very much, as you may suppose, my legs were so badly cramped; so I watched my chance, slipped out of the cloak, and ran down stairs as fast as I could.

"'You need not wear crape for me just yet, if you please,' said Pet, saucily shaking her bell.

"Tom's family made him a nice visit, then went to their several homes again, all very well satisfied that the step-mother was a good cat, after all. Tom still lives in the garret, where he is very happy indeed, although he sometimes has the rheumatism after damp weather."

The evening closed pleasantly after the Cricket's story was finished.

The Teapot was brushing up her wits to think of something the turtle had told her, when they were making that long journey together from China; but she was not destined to tell the story, for a misfortune happened that threw the deepest gloom over the whole Club. The Cricket went out in a snow-storm and wet his feet, after which imprudence he had an attack of brain-fever. The others met every night, as usual, but it was not for any amusement as before,—they now wore gloomy, anxious faces, and wagged their heads solemnly over the poor Cricket's illness. As for the Kettle, he sighed so deeply all the time that he kept boiling dry, which caused the maidservant Hulda much vexation.

At one time the Cricket's life was despaired of, but, fortunately, they sent for a new doctor, who put a bandage of cold water upon the patient's head, which had a very good effect. The doctor also bled him in one foot, and cut off a feeler, so that at last, to the great joy of his friends, he recovered.

When he was well enough to appear on the hearth, the Club were delighted to see him again, although he was very much altered, his face being thin, and his head shaved so that he was obliged to wear a red cap and tassel.

"I am very glad to be able to appear here once more," he said in a feeble voice, "for I wish to introduce some new members, who may tell us something interesting. They are the travelled

Spider, the ambitious Wasp, and the disappointed Caterpillar."

How far these new members may add to the existing attractions of the Kettle Club, the author is unable at present to state, but she hopes next Christmas we may hear more of them all.

THE END.

Cambridge: Press of John Wilson and Son.

www.ingramcontent.com/pod-product-compliance
Lightning Source LLC
Chambersburg PA
CBHW020231030726
47497CB00009B/3051